Stormchild

Pacific Passion, Book 1

These elements have no desire to be tamed...

As the new traveling doctor for the Pacific Inside Passage settlements, Matthew Jentry balances dual roles for his water-shifter people—caring for their health as a human-trained physician, and for their spiritual needs as a shaman.

Distractions of the female kind are not on his agenda, but his magical bloodline makes him a target for every marriage-minded woman within range. There's something about the mysterious Laurin Marshall, though, that he finds far too enticing. It's just as well that it's time for him to move on.

Laurin thought she had perfected her guise as a mild-mannered teacher, but the sexual fireworks she and Matt touch off are threatening to blow her cover out of the water. Luckily it's time for her to catch the boat to her next assignment.

When she discovers she'll be sailing with Matt, she realizes there's only one thing more dangerous than their unforgettable one-night stand—being trapped with him on a boat that gives "riding out the storm" a whole new meaning...

Warning: Contains strong sexual currents and powerful waves of desire that break down inhibitions. Recommended only for those able to navigate through extremely steamy situations, on land and at sea.

Stormy Seduction

Pacific Passion, Book 2

Sensual water shifters meet volatile air shifters—there's a storm coming.

As morning-afters go, this one is looking pretty bright. Both air shifter Laurin Marshal and water shifter/shaman Matthew Jentry are aware, though, that trouble won't be long in coming. And they're right—before they've barely begun to work out the details of their mystical bond, the People of the Air find them to challenge Laurin's right to choose Matt as her mate.

Fending off Laurin's would-be suitors is easier than Matt anticipated, but there's another dilemma still to face. His own people. Laurin is just beginning to trust that his heart and body are completely hers, a radical change after she's spent the past two years alone and on the run. What will happen when his skittish, innocent partner encounters the playful, sensual— even lusty—ways of the Otter Clan?

Especially since they are arriving at the peak of the traditional summer solstice fertility rituals. And tradition demands they be the main attraction...

Warning: Incoming extreme passion yielding one otherworldly adventure. Don't let the book length fool you— there's enough heat in this story to challenge global warming. Four plus two equals one ceremony so explosive it may throw the earth off its axis.

Silent Storm

Pacific Passion, Book 3

Love speaks volumes without a single word.

In the months they've traveled together, Laurin Marshall and Matt Jentry's attraction has grown beyond spectacular sexual passion into a deeper emotional connection. Still, Laurin wrestles with one last question: how a water shifter and an air shifter can possibly find permanent common ground.

Matt is content to wait patiently for Laurin to realize he has no desire to change her sky-borne nature. Until a giant golden eagle touches down on the *Stormchild* and tips the delicate balance of more than just the boat.

Laurin's obvious affection for the newcomer comes as a shock. And so does the flash of jealousy that interferes with his shamanic ability to heal the man's malady. While Matt struggles to balance his conflicted responsibilities, Laurin attempts to reconcile her undeniable feelings for one of her kind with her desire for Matt.

Somewhere between the ocean depths and the mountaintops, they need to find a love strong enough to call them both home to the *Stormchild*.

Warning: Familiar lovers (hot) with old rivals (hotter) and a wild curse-melting ménage (hottest yet). Get ready for one exotic paranormal that will make you look to the skies and sea with longing.

Look for these titles by
Vivian Arend

Now Available:

Storm Swept

Vivian Arend

SAMHAIN
PUBLISHING

Samhain Publishing, Ltd.
11821 Mason Montgomery Road, 4B
Cincinnati, OH 45249
www.samhainpublishing.com

Storm Swept
Print ISBN: 978-1-60928-472-5
Stormchild Copyright © 2012 by Vivian Arend
Stormy Seduction Copyright © 2012 by Vivian Arend
Silent Storm Copyright © 2012 by Vivian Arend

Editing by Anne Scott
Cover by Angela Waters

Stormchild, ISBN 978-1-60504-956-4
First Samhain Publishing, Ltd. electronic publication: May 2010
Stormy Seduction, ISBN 978-1-60928-423-7
First Samhain Publishing, Ltd. electronic publication: April 2011
Silent Storm, ISBN 978-1-60928-455-8
First Samhain Publishing, Ltd. electronic publication: May 2011
First Samhain Publishing, Ltd. print publication: April 2012

Contents

Stormchild

Dedication

To my dad, who took me out in my first sailboat years ago on the IJsselmeer in Holland. You started me thinking life is an adventure to be experienced fully.

And to my hubby who takes me out in kayaks, canoes, rowboats and other watercraft to prove many times over that the adventure is never done.

Chapter One

His lack of arousal would have been embarrassing if it wasn't so damn amusing.

The gold-tinged light of sunset cast shadowy fingers over the half-naked bodies dancing around the fire pit. Hips twisted and torsos shimmied. Reflected firelight flickered off warm skin and firm muscles and something ached deep in his soul. Matthew Jentry reclined on one elbow in the sand and accepted the honor of his people's traditional tribal farewell.

Two weeks at this settlement had provided plenty of opportunities to witness the innate sensuality of the People of the Sea. His first concern had been medical checkups for a tribe who lived far from the easy access to care in Vancouver or Victoria.

The matriarch had other goals.

He spotted her across the fire ring, staring with a hint of amusement in her smile. As another of the lithe young women danced nearer, leaning to display her ample assets to their best advantage, Matthew laughed inside.

Yes, he knew it was traditional for travelers to share pleasure with the locals. He knew it was considered an honor to provide such a service, especially to one like himself who was both a magical and modern healer.

But he wanted more. No matter how tempting the offers

before him, he had started this position the way he meant to continue. Alone. Until he found the one to complement him and make his true mission a reality, he had no intention of hopping into bed with anyone. After a dry spell of six months, his urge for sex still lay dormant.

The dance concluded and he applauded along with the elders around him, accepting pats on the back from the men as they shuffled off to enjoy the barbeque pit and containers of sweet cider cooling in buckets by the surf. Mama Tanis cornered him before he vanished to safety with the old men.

For a large woman she moved with amazing speed.

"You enjoyed the dance?" She stared at him, eyes filled with wisdom. She was old—far older than the medical records in the town office showed.

"I did. Thank you for honoring me before I head to the next village. I cherish the time I have had with you." He bowed low in respect.

She shook a finger in his face. "You say that, but I think you're following your own way, not Mama T's. Why do I see you with the old men who have no juice left in their veins? I can entertain them with stories. You should be on the beach with the young people, living and laughing and loving."

"Mama T—"

"Oh no, you avoided all our entertainments the whole time you stayed with us. You worked from sunrise to dark, and even now when you're leaving, you think of ways to avoid play."

He lifted a brow. "Perhaps I am too old and juiceless myself to want to inflict my company on the young people."

The woman shook with her laughter. "Too juiceless? The only thing you are guilty of is being too cautious, my friend. I will stop taunting you. This night is for you, enjoy it as you wish." She leaned forward and her dark eyes bore into him.

"But I will tell you this. Sometimes what you seek is closer than you imagine, and found only when you stop looking."

A shiver raced over his skin as she spoke. A prophecy? An omen? There was no way of knowing. The People of the Sea were rich in power in many ways. He bowed again, grasping her hand and kissing her knuckles. His actions drew a chuckle from her lips.

"You're a bad boy to tease Mama T."

He winked at her, and she shook her head and smiled.

Matt stepped back, ready to rejoin the men, when it hit him. *Oh hell, he'd forgotten.* "I need to apologize. You asked me to examine one of your people. She never showed up for her appointment. I tried to make another slot available but was told she had gone on a camping trip. The high school students went on a field trip to do biology research, or something. I'll have to see her next time I visit."

The matriarch folded her lips together into a firm line. "I should have known. She insists there is no issue, that she doesn't need a shaman's help." She sighed. "As you said, it will have to wait. I'm going to give her a piece of my mind when I see her. I told her myself I wanted her to keep the appointment."

Matthew stopped in amazement. "I've rarely heard of any troubles with youths challenging the hierarchies of our people. How could she ignore a direct command from you? What's the problem that she'd flout her matriarch to avoid seeing me?"

Mama Tanis planted her fists on her wide hips. "The girl can't shift. We know she's got shifter blood, but we've never seen her make the change."

He wandered down the beach, Mama T's gaze burning his back. A chuckle escaped him again. The world of academia he'd exchanged for the world of the mystic created a study in contrasts. Conflicting as it seemed at times, both were full of truths. Germs and viruses caused disease, but so did evil spirits and curses. His challenge as shaman was to bring the two worlds into harmony, no matter how strange the blend appeared.

The light faded from the sky, twilight's streaks coloring the horizon over the ocean. Matt paced carefully, his bare feet comfortable against the still-warm sands. The puzzle presented by the matriarch tugged at his mind again like an undercurrent dragging him out of his path. A shifter who couldn't shift—for the People of the Sea it would be like never learning to walk. Until they were as at home in the water as on land, a person would never truly fit in.

On impulse, he angled farther down the beach toward where the young people gathered around a large bonfire. Perhaps he'd be able to spot the girl amongst her friends, get a feel for her trouble without frightening her. Although he couldn't imagine why she was scared to see the shaman. The strains of guitar music rose on the air and ahead he spotted couples cuddled together around the heat of the blaze.

His gaze caught on a smaller circle farther inland, a group of laughing mothers watching protectively from their beach chairs a few metres away. The children played an intricate game involving switching positions and hiding a shiny shell of abalone. A woman knelt in their midst, her head thrown back in laughter, straight blonde hair tousled around her shoulders.

His body tightened. There was something more provocative in her uninhibited moment of delight than in all the sensual beauty he'd seen during the earlier dance. He watched with a growing ache in his groin as she joined a child in the outer circle and the game carried on around them.

Dark eyes, light skin. She must be a visitor to the people.

He'd never seen a fair-haired shifter among the orca clans, and Mama T would have told him about such an anomaly. The woman hadn't been one of the many of the settlement on whom he'd done a routine physical exam during the past two weeks. He rejoiced he'd avoided having to give her an examination when the mere sight of her heated his blood and drove his desire insanely high.

He had to meet her.

Another burst of giggles rose from the children as he changed directions to enter the circle. Childish voices cried out in greeting. No matter where he went, it was the little ones who made his heart sing the loudest, and he longed for the day he would have his own. He would sire them and raise them *and* they would remain a family. He swore this would happen, no matter what traditions were held amongst the shamans.

He exchanged hugs, accepted kisses and waved a greeting to the mothers who watched cautiously. A few blushed, but most looked pleased to have their offspring gain his attention. Then he slowly turned his focus to her. Savoring the moment, prolonging the time until their eyes met.

Midnight-filled orbs stared back, the curve of her cheek creamy white in contrast with her dark lashes. Her full lips drew him, the bottom one glistening where she'd licked it seconds earlier. He dropped his gaze slowly down her torso, not even trying to hide how attractive he found her curves and modest shift.

"You gonna play?" Small hands pulled him to the sand ahead of his response. He sank into position gratefully.

A mischievous smile tugged at the corner of the woman's mouth as she looked him over. "You know how to play the game?"

He knelt upright in the middle of the circle and nodded.

Surprise flashed in her eyes before he covered his face with his hands and the chanting began. Around him, small bodies moved and singsong voices echoed with the tune of a thousand years of tradition. When they stopped, another of the contrasts between the People of the Sea and the children of the human world grew apparent.

Utter silence surrounded him.

He removed his hands and let his eyes adjust to the dim light offered by the distant fire. All the childish voices were still, hands quiet, faces blank. Matt observed carefully before moving toward one of the pairs of children. They stared back with soft smiles, and he grinned. He traced their arms with a light tickling motion. They never moved.

A giggle broke free behind him and he spun. The culprit calmed her expression seconds too late and Matt crawled across the sand on his hands and knees, growling like a ferocious beast. The others laughed as he focused his attention on the noisemaker and her partner.

Oh sweet Lord, his mysterious woman sat behind the child.

He froze for a moment until her flashing eyes taunted him. Brushing the little girl's arms gave far too little opportunity to brace himself for the next step. The blonde sat motionless, moonlight turning her hair into a glowing beacon. He took his time, running his palms along her silky flesh instead of using his fingertips like he had on the children. The caress of skin on skin made his mouth go dry and his body harden further with desire.

It was a child's game and he was getting turned on. There was no mercy in the world.

The child in her lap shifted and knocked against his arm. His fingers grazed the side of the woman's breast and she sucked in a gasp of air. He wanted to ignore the fact her nipple hardened instantly, but his gaze had locked on her torso like on a target.

Where the hell had she been for the past two weeks? Because all his righteous plans about remaining celibate were floating out on the evening tide. If there was any justice, any magic in the world, they were meant to be together. Even if it was just for one night.

Chapter Two

Laurin cursed her libido for exposing her need so clearly to the visitor. She didn't do casual. She didn't. She might want to scratch her itch, but certainly not with someone she'd never met before.

And maybe if she recited that lie often enough she'd come to believe it. There was nothing casual about what she wanted from the dark stranger kneeling close by. Only the children of the settlement surrounding them stopped her from pressing him back to the sand and crawling on top to ride him into oblivion.

When he pulled the hidden shell from under her partner's arm, squeals of delight rose around them. The little girl crawled forward, pausing to drop a kiss on the man's cheek before taking her place in the center of the circle. Voices rose for a moment and Laurin was caught between horror and fascination as she realized he had to take his place in the pairs.

With her.

She ignored the fact her pussy grew instantly wet and instead inched forward to make room. He settled intimately behind her, his thighs surrounding and caging her. One arm tucked under her ribcage as he leaned her torso back and her breath caught in her throat.

Firm muscles were everywhere. In his arms, his thighs, his

body. The simple fact their bodies touched made a shiver trace up her spine and goose bumps rise on her skin.

He laughed softly. "Cold?" The whisper tickled her ear, as he brushed his lips against the lobe. A hint of moisture adhered as he licked and a brief shudder shook her from head to toe. "I can warm you up. If you're interested..."

The game in front of them had resumed. Laurin was grateful for a moment's distraction. *Oh damn, oh damn, oh damn.* She had to decide, and now. Did she want to go off with this stranger, as delectable as he seemed? Tomorrow morning she headed to the next of her one-month teaching assignments in another settlement. He was obviously an orca shifter returning from the outside world.

She'd never taken advantage of the sexual favors offered by the People. After spending the past two years traveling from settlement to settlement along the Pacific Inside Passage, all the tribes knew she taught the children to the best of her abilities and otherwise stayed strictly alone. Even the oversexed otter folk hadn't managed to convince her to play around, although they had come the closest to tempting her.

Until now.

The firm clasp of his arm warned her a spilt second before he moved closer. Oh God, his erection pressed into the seam of her butt, heat scorching through the material of his jeans and the thin cotton of her dress. He adjusted his arm slightly until her breasts rested on his forearm, his hand clasping the side of her torso. Then he moved his thumb in a gentle stroke and she moaned with need.

"My name is Matt."

The butterfly softness of his words caressed her ear. She wiggled and an involuntary squeak escaped her. Childish laughter drew her attention back to the game as the seeker

19

approached to discover the hidden shell. They didn't have it, but there was no way Laurin wanted anyone to know what else had risen between them. She forced a small smile as the little girl made a quick search. Matt squeezed them together, his cock a firebrand against her. Somehow he twisted his hand under her arm to allow his fingers to slip into her tank-top sleeve. Skin touched skin. She held her breath as images filled her mind of the other places she wanted skin on skin. With him.

And that was her answer, wasn't it?

Perhaps it was for the best. With her leaving in the morning there would be little time for personal discovery. They could enjoy what looked to be a spectacular physical attraction without having to deal with future questions about where she came from and who she really was.

Sex. Plain and simple. She could do that. Right?

He stroked again with his thumb and her pussy creamed involuntarily. Plain and simple? She doubted it. Hotter than Hades? Oh yeah.

The game ended abruptly as the mothers clapped their hands, cajoling their young ones to head for home. The group rose to their feet, children milling about bestowing goodnight hugs before joining the exodus. Stars filled the sky overhead, the ocean waves carrying a lullaby across the settlement. Laurin nodded back at the polite bows directed her way. She knew the families appreciated her ability to cover everything from ABCs to trigonometry. The People of the Sea lived an isolated lifestyle, but their children still learned of the outside world. The orca clan was one of the larger settlements, only four hours from Vancouver Island by powerboat. They had a large enough population she might even be able to convince the department of education a full-time teacher would be a worthwhile investment.

A smooth caress on her arm reminded her that this time when the children left, she wasn't alone.

"You're not shivering anymore." He hesitated, and she hurried to reassure him. Now she'd decided, there was no way she'd miss this opportunity.

She turned to face him, staring into surprisingly blue eyes. With his dark skin and hair, she'd expected the predominately dark shades common among the orca people. Fascination filled his expression as he gazed at her lips. Instinctively she licked them, and he groaned, wrapping his arms around her. As she settled into his embrace, something softened in her core and desire flooded her body.

"Heat me up," she whispered, raising her hands to cup his face. A soft kiss. Another. She planted delicate caresses on his lips until he snatched her closer and assumed control. He consumed her. Feasted on her. He slid his mouth down to suckle on the pulse point throbbing at the juncture of her neck and shoulder. Cupping her ass in his hands, he dragged her hard against his body. Her mound connected with his erection and he lifted her, rubbing them together. Her last lucid thought was they still stood on the beach, in plain view of the whole clan.

He growled deep in his throat and swung her up, marching into the shadows as he continued to offer his lips in worship. She closed her eyes and blindly accepted wherever he took her. Blindly accepted the wonders of what his mouth did to her. It went beyond kisses. A world of desire passed between them and the only connection point was their lips.

He ducked low, and she opened her eyes to find they were in a wall tent. As he lowered her to the mattress she glanced around. There were few personal possessions in the square dwelling. A simple trunk stood in the corner next to an empty desk. She lived in a similar space, and all her belongings were already packed in preparation for the morning.

Preparation. *Shit.*

"Do you have a condom?" She pressed on his chest to separate them, even as her fingers curled involuntarily to clasp the soft cotton of his shirt.

An inexplicable expression floated across Matt's face before he hurried away to swing open his trunk and rummage in its depths. She sat up to watch him. It was reassuring he didn't haul protection out of his back pocket like he hoped this would happen. A twinge of doubt at her actions hit, but before she could act, he turned in triumph. Their eyes met, and she was lost.

She had to have him.

Matt flicked on the small lantern beside the desk, and a dim glow filled the tent. A hazy, smoky light that turned his dusky skin even darker as he approached to kneel before her. He stared into her eyes for the longest time. The brilliant blue of his irises burned into her like an x-ray and she felt exposed. Every desire—and right now she had a lot of them—laid bare for him to examine. She had to drop her gaze.

Instead she watched from under heavily lidded lashes as he unbuttoned his shirt. Muscles carved from obsidian graced his torso, and she reached without thinking to stroke the ridges of his abdomen. Hmm, soft skin, rock-solid base. She slid forward on the mattress to press both palms against the heat radiating from him.

"What's your name, my ray of moonshine?" His voice teased all the dark parts in her soul with needs she'd never dreamed she had. She swallowed hard as he shrugged his shirt off and reached to unbutton her dress.

"Laurin."

His gaze remained locked on her body as the edges of her cotton shift separated. The cool breeze of the ocean snuck in the tent flaps to brush her skin.

"A beautiful name." He stroked his knuckles along the edge of her bra and her nipples tightened to the point of pain. "Laurin, I thank you for the gift of sharing pleasure with me tonight."

The air rippled around them and she held her breath. Something magical had begun, and she was powerless to stop it. Perhaps this was what always happened during a sexual encounter with the People of the Sea. She wouldn't know.

Matt leaned toward her and she met him halfway. Their lips connected as his hand slipped forward to cup her bra-clad breast. His flavor, smoky sweet, tickled her taste buds as she accepted his seeking tongue. Nips and licks, and open-mouthed kisses followed, while his thumb traced wicked circles around her nipple. She wanted to stay like this forever, the tender touch of his firm mouth against hers. He snuck his other hand around her neck to direct the angle of her mouth. Laurin groaned, wanting him closer. Wanting to be consumed by his taste, consumed by his heat. He stroked his tongue along her teeth and over the roof of her mouth and she answered by sucking lightly.

When he left her lips and moved to her lace-covered breast with his mouth, a soft sigh escaped her. She arched under him, inching closer until her thighs bumped his hips. Her heated core nestled against his abdomen and the gentle abrasion set her clit throbbing.

The world slowed to nothing but her sense of touch. An aching heat shot to her womb from where he suckled at her breast, melting fingers of pleasure spreading leisurely. He moved his hand to her thigh, smoothing the inside of her leg until he cupped her core.

"Oh damn, you're wet." His fingers stroked over her panties. A firm controlled touch that teased and enticed. She opened her legs farther and moaned in protest when he pulled away. Wordlessly he stripped off her dress, removed her panties and bra and arranged her on the mattress to his liking. He undressed quickly, then stood over her. The admiration on his face was echoed in the admiration shown by his body, his cock jutting from his groin. A whimper escaped as she fought the urge to taste the pearly bead clinging to the rigid tip.

"Please..." She stared at him, unable to complete her statement of need. She grew feverish waiting for him to stop looking and start touching.

The pale glow of her beauty wrapped around his heart as much as around his body. As Matt gazed at Laurin, laid out like some kind of exotic feast on his bed, he wondered when he had lost control of the situation.

The magic filling the room was more powerful than he'd ever experienced. Sexual pleasure was a strong catalyst for shaman skills, but of this intensity? The unreasonable concentration of passion he felt scared him. Made him hesitate and wonder if it was safe to continue. He sat beside her with care and laid his hand on her chest, his fingers splaying out as he opened himself to his mystic side. It wasn't an invasive search, only a surface questioning of her innate skills.

Nothing.

Nothing came to him except the overwhelming desire to drive into her body and never leave. Laurin moaned, a small noise deep in her throat, and he lost all interest in solving the mystery of why the room blazed with energy. He'd formally accepted her offered gift, now was time to enjoy each other. They could seek answers later.

He covered her with his naked body. He sucked in a quick breath at the rightness of the sensation, heat to heat, hard to soft. Lip to lip as he took her mouth again. Honeysuckle sweet, submissive under him, Laurin lifted her hands to stroke his back with a whisper-light touch. Her legs fell open to allow him to nestle closer. His erection wept where it rested against her belly, and involuntarily he rocked his hips, shifting them lower. The motion dragged his shaft through her soft curls and moisture from her pussy coated his cock.

He kissed his way down her body, worshipping her breasts, nuzzling the underside of the sweet curves until she squirmed. A trail of kisses descended farther, stopping only to lap at her bellybutton. She gave a soft giggle when he dipped his tongue into the indent, and he leaned up on one elbow to smile at her.

"I love the sound of your laugh."

Her dark eyes twinkled at him. "I love what you're doing to me."

"Hmm." He kissed her belly, his gaze locked on hers. "Any requests?"

She stared back wide-eyed. "Don't stop," she whispered.

The fragrance rising from between her legs tormented him and he could wait no longer. "Your command is my wish, my lady."

He glanced at the pale curls covering her mound, moisture clinging to them. He drew in a deep breath to fill his head and his lungs with her scent before dropping his mouth to kiss her intimately.

Had he imagined she tasted of honeysuckle? No, far sweeter. Her flavor burst forth like an exquisite wine and he savored each sip. Parting her curls with his fingers to expose pale pink folds, he traced delicate circles with his tongue. Laurin quivered beneath his mouth, her nether lips flowering open as he laved again and again, lapping the cream leaving her body. The moisture, that even now, prepared her body for their joining.

The erect tip of her clitoris peeked out from its protective hood and he drew it into his mouth and suckled gently. She cried out, then relaxed under him, tangling her fingers in his hair. He hummed against her core, slipping a finger into her depths to test her readiness. A wave of lust raced over him as her passage squeezed so tightly he had to concentrate on not coming right then and there like an inexperienced youth.

"Oh damn, Laurin. Just...damn."

She raised her hips, demanding his attention and he gave it, whole-heartedly. A second finger joined the first and he stroked the front of her sheath with a curling touch. He licked and sucked in turns until her body responded like a wave breaking on the shore, exploding against the rocks and flaring up into the cool night air. Laurin arched hard, her head thrashing from side to side, small moans of delight escaping her lips.

He continued to touch and caress, softer now, more and more gently until the aftershocks faded away. When their gazes met she had tears in her eyes and something inside his heart twisted. Matt rose and kissed her, their bodies tangling together as she twined her fingers in his hair and held their mouths together. He rolled them over, loving the sensation of her weight resting on top of him. Then he clasped her hips, squeezing her muscular butt cheeks. The heavy weight of his erection rested between her open legs. When she slid up slightly to kiss her way along his temple, the hot wet tip of his cock pressed against her slick opening.

They both froze.

The dire urge to thrust confused the hell out of him. He was the one who didn't want to leave children behind like a trail of foam in his wake. He was the one who should be getting out of this position and sheathing up. It made no sense, but he was powerless to move. Frozen in place as he used every bit of his power to remain still and not bury himself to the hilt.

Laurin was the one who swore and slid to safety. She sat on his abdomen, the pulsing heat of her core smearing a line of moisture on his skin.

"Condom. Oh God, please, I don't want to stop, but you've got to—"

"I've got it." He spun her again, dropping her flat on the mattress, taking her mouth in a tender caress that grew harder and more needy by the second. He squeezed her breasts together and lapped from side to side, nipping at the now bright red tips until she dragged his head away. He rose over her and for one awful, dreadful, marvelous moment he was once again lined up bareback with her welcoming passage. Their eyes met and he swore.

"Damn it, I want you so badly. Like this, skin touching skin." He rocked his hips and his cock nestled a little deeper. He closed his eyes and gritted his teeth together. Oh fuck, he needed to stop but the thought was killing him. Why was everything in him crying for them to come together unhindered by anything unnatural?

"Please not without... I can't, I just can't." Again Laurin was the one who found the strength to stop them. She wiggled from under him, whimpering piteously. His magic flashed—even as she left him he sensed she wept for his touch without the barrier. She wanted him as much as he wanted her.

No—needed. This went beyond want. This was off the scale

of desire and pleasure. Somehow joining with her had become as necessary as breathing and having the sun rise in the morning. Dazed, mind clouded, the rustle of foil broke through his distorted hearing. He managed to mindlessly open the package but his very soul protested his attempts to put on the condom. Laurin moved to help, and the touch of her hands on his aching cock was like the first flush of dawn's light after a stormy winter night. Every cell in his body yearned for her and as soon as she rolled the latex over his erection he clasped her back into his embrace.

They scrambled together, half-sitting, half-lying and then in one frantic motion they joined. She sank onto him with a soul-emptying keen of delight. It tightened his groin and sharpened his senses to everything they shared. Her breasts rocked against his chest, her turgid nipples scratching his sensitive skin. Her soft belly rubbed his abdomen and she wrapped her arms around his neck, clinging to him. She pumped hard onto his shaft, driving it deeper into her welcoming warmth. He kissed her frantically, attempting to silently apologize for his lack of control even as he took back the lead, grasping her hips to lift and lower her again and again. The sweet cream between them eased his way through her tight clasp. Tongues tangled and thrust together in imitation of their hips.

Suddenly there was nothing but impending fireworks and lightning strikes breaking across their bodies. He brought her down hard one last time, flexing his hips to drive them as close together as possible as the first pulses of her orgasm fluttered around him. His mind emptied with his seed, the sensation of being in her arms and in her body so good and so right, words failed him.

Breathlessly he waited until the tremors racking them both faded to something on the lower end of the Richter scale. He dropped a kiss on her shoulder, the heat of her skin welding its way through him like a branding iron.

By the time he could move again, they both shivered in the cool night air. He pulled back the sheets and lowered her tenderly to the mattress surface. Laurin's eyes remained shut, a dusting of tears painting her lashes. He kissed them away before leaving her briefly to deal with the condom.

Then he returned and wrapped himself like a blanket around her, physically unable to let the sensation of her skin touching his stop even a moment before the dawn broke.

Chapter Three

It was somehow distasteful and very trite. Yet when she woke before Matt, her first thought was to find a way to sneak out of his grasp and get to the harbor as quickly and quietly as possible.

Still, she stared at his face for a full minute, memorizing the lines, the firm bone structure. Whatever else had happened last night, she didn't regret her actions. Or at least she wouldn't if she made it out of his tent without disturbing him. She didn't need any early-morning complications. Rolling cautiously, Laurin slipped from under his muscular arm and slid off the bed. Her dress lay across the back of the chair, and she inched it over her head in an instant.

Then she was out the tent flap, returning to her own place, hoping to avoid any of the early-rising locals on their way fishing. She didn't need a lengthy tête-à-tête with anyone about why she still wore last night's clothing.

The crisp morning breeze filled her nostrils like a refreshing spring rain. It was always difficult to say goodbye to a community, but heading to a new settlement excited her as well. Laurin ducked into her own tent to change into travel gear and grab her day bag. Someone had already picked up her main suitcase and she quickly prepared for the coming trip. She wondered briefly who Mama T had conned into giving her a ride to her next teaching assignment. Most of the time she ended up on slow-moving barges or supply vessels. Occasionally a speedboat, but that convenience was far more rare. All she knew was that by nine a.m. she had to get to the harbor.

She spent her spare time on a rocky outcrop overlooking the settlement, staring at the ocean and wondering why the taste of Matt lingered in her mouth. Last night had amazed her, overwhelmed her.

Scared her to death.

She'd been so close to making love unprotected. That wasn't her way. Something about the combination of her and Matt made her lose control—the passion in the room had been off the charts. She wished she could crawl back into his arms and ask for another round. The magic they'd shared had been unlike any previous sexual experience.

She laughed at herself. Two years of hiding from her heritage, and she'd been close to throwing it all away on a whim. Part of the reason she'd left the mountains and come to the ocean was to escape from her supposed destiny. The People of the Air were good people. She just didn't want to end up the partner of anyone who thought they met all the requirements of some ancient mystical prophecy. She wasn't ready to settle down and she'd left before anyone forced her to make a dire mistake.

Still, she missed shifting. The need to remain hidden had required staying in human form. It had been far too long since she'd soared through the air and she missed riding the currents and gliding above the clouds. Above her head the sky grew brighter, tinged with a harsh red. A storm gathered strength in the distance. She smelt it on the air, the electrical charge sharp in her nostrils. Her journey from this settlement would be less than idyllic. The wind shifted, now blowing out toward the sea, and she rose. Time for daydreaming was over. Whoever she was hitching a ride with would have to hurry to stay ahead of the weather.

The well-worn boards of the dock bounced underfoot as she strode to the waiting boats. She watched one of the village men load her trunk onto a yacht, and Laurin breathed a sigh of relief she wouldn't be trapped on the boat anchored at the end of the harbor, a scrap barge, going at a snail's pace through the Inside Passage.

Laurin whistled as she caught a closer look at the nearer ship. Her lines were clean and trim, sparkling in the sunshine reflecting off the water. She was a beautiful craft—single mast, rigged to allow an experienced sailor to handle her solo with ease. Laurin bet an inboard engine would be tucked beneath for those days the ocean turned to a sheet of glass or for a day like today when getting ahead of the wind meant safety. With delight, she spotted a kayak carrier jutting off the back, her own well-loved cedar strip already strapped in place beside a gorgeous Kevlar single seater, the brilliant red of its sides glowing like the sun.

Nice. *Very* nice.

The boat drew her like a magnet, and in a moment she was by the vessel's side, stroking a hand along the gunwale, squatting to see the name painted across the prow.

Stormchild.

She crawled aboard, completely mesmerized by the craft. Two comfortable seats in the open stern would allow passengers to face the water. She pressed her nose to the window of the covered pilothouse to peer at the helm. Exquisite woodwork filled the space, the cherry red tones bringing warmth and beauty to every detail.

"Ahem." Mama Tanis stood on the dock with her heavy fists

planted on her hips. Laurin straightened with embarrassment. Invading another person's boat, no matter how attractive, was uncommonly rude.

"I'm sorry, I—"

"I see you've discovered the ride I arranged."

Laurin let her delight shine through. "Oh Mama T, I love you."

Hearty rolls of laughter sprang from the matriarch's throat, and Laurin joined in, suddenly feeling wonderfully alive. The wind whipped her hair across her eyes and she pulled it back, tucking it up with an elastic from her pocket.

The matriarch stared for a moment. She nodded as if in approval. "You're ready early."

Laurin hopped the gunwales and returned to the travel bag she'd dropped on the platform and bowed carefully. "There's no use in waiting. Tide turns in thirty minutes. If I'm here we can leave as soon as the owners are ready." Mama Tanis raised a brow, as if waiting. Laurin shrugged uncertainly. "Is something wrong?"

"I fail to understand how a bright young woman like you can be so bullheaded and lacking in common sense."

Laurin frowned. She glanced around in confusion. "What have I done?"

"Such a complete lack of curiosity. You haven't even asked who the pilot is for your vessel."

The traveling bag slung over her shoulder, Laurin stepped aside to let the man who had brought her case on board pass her. He nodded politely then hurried up the dock and out of the gathering wind. "I'm pleased with whatever arrangements you've made for me."

Mama Tanis chuckled loudly. "Really? You seemed to have

had troubles with other earlier arrangements I made for you."

The appointment. Damn, she'd hoped to get away before Mama T discovered she'd ditched the checkup. "I'm fine. I appreciate your concern, but I'm fine."

They stared at each other. The other-worldliness of the people rolled out from the matriarch and Laurin stiffened her spine. She would not succumb to the mystical—accept it, yes, but never did she consent to let the animal nature rule her human side. She didn't want anyone to know her powers. She hesitantly braced a wall between them, not allowing the orca clan leader to read any sign of her talents.

"You resist? How can you…?" Mama's voice was a whisper, shock lacing her words.

Laurin thought quickly. "I'm just a visitor. Your authority can't force me like it would a local under your protection." She dipped her head respectfully, cursing she'd had to show a hint of her own abilities.

Soft chuckles broke from the older woman. "So hesitant to share. I will say again, sometimes what you need is much closer than you think."

A deep rich laugh rang out that Laurin's body instantly recognized. She scanned the dock frantically, trying to see where the hell he was when a shiver teased her spine.

His voice boomed directly behind her. "Mama T, are you still taunting me? What I need is not cryptic words, but my passenger."

Laurin turned in time to see Matt pop out from the wheelhouse, his bright blue eyes flashing his surprise as they raked her from head to toe.

The close quarters of the boat grew even closer after three hours, and Laurin felt the tension like a gathering storm. They spoke little, both distracted with their own thoughts. The graceful vessel moved slowly through a dangerous section of shoals and sandbars. Matt concentrated diligently at the helm as he studied the radar scanner and the map spread beside him. The waves had grown in height as time passed, the sky slate grey and heavy with the coming moisture. Whitecaps peaked higher and higher to splash over the boat's sides, soaking the deck.

Laurin paced to the door and splayed her fingers against the glass. The cold moisture condensed on the pane did nothing to ease the heat rising in her body. Something inside her longed to break free and soar into the wild wind. She wanted to challenge with wing and claw to reach the calm above the storm. The urge to shift grew increasingly frantic and it took everything in her to fight it down. Shifting wasn't possible right now. She had to resist.

She turned from studying the darkening sky to stare instead at Matt's profile. He was every bit as gorgeous now in the day as last night. Oh God, last night. Her skin tightened, her breasts ached. The wheelhouse was too small to contain the two of them *and* her memories of them tangled intimately together.

Matt cleared his throat. "This is going to sound strange, but could you please stop? I can't concentrate with you..." He jerked the wheel to the side and the scrape of sand rubbing along their starboard side sounded briefly. The ship rocked between the unbalancing waves and their narrow escape of the shoal.

Rubbing. She wanted to rub on him. This time, with no time limits about when they needed to stop. No fears of being discovered. Just time to explore his body, admire the firm muscles and let him—

35

The motor cut off, breaking her reverie. Suddenly he clasped her arms and spoke directly in her face. "Laurin! Enough. Please. Go below into the main saloon, or the galley, and let me navigate through this mess before we get in real trouble. The storm will peak soon and I need to find a safe harbor."

She fled like a startled bird.

When he was out of sight, her overwhelming sense of urgency weakened. The need to touch him remained, but at least once again her mind was her own. The motor restarted, the familiar hum calming her. She put on a kettle of water for coffee, latching it safely in place against the rocking motion of the ship. Doing something normal in the midst of the chaos was what she needed. Laurin drew a long, slow breath.

What the hell was happening? Ever since she'd spotted him on the boat, the feverish desire to roll herself all over him had grown to epic proportions.

Back on the dock she hadn't said a word of protest. Hadn't let even a blush indicate she'd already known who he was when Mama T introduced them. A wry smile hit her lips as she dug through the cupboards of the galley to find the supplies she needed. The rich scent of coffee beans hit her nose and eased her soul a little. She *hadn't* known who he was, and that was the point. In some ways it was comical her one-night stand happened with the only man in the settlement who wasn't staying.

A shaman. She had to pick a damn shaman for her first sexual encounter with the People of the Sea. She snorted in derision. If you had to screw up, screw up big. He was the most likely candidate to be able to unravel her secrets. Although letting him discover all the things she hid potentially meant a lot of fun. They'd need at least a few more rounds in bed, and possibly even...

She jerked herself upright. *What the hell was up with her hormones?*

Laurin enjoyed sex. Not in the "need it, gotta have it" daily kinda way like her caffeine or dark chocolate. But ever since she'd laid eyes on Matthew Jentry, she'd been like a homing pigeon trying to come back to roost. She imagined his capable hands on the wheel, guiding them through the dangerous passage. Better yet to imagine his hands on her body, smoothing up her torso to cup her breasts, his dark skin contrasting with her fairness. He'd roll his thumbs over her nipples while supporting the aching globes in his palms.

Laurin leaned back on the short countertop and closed her eyes. God, she could almost feel it, the tingling sensation from her tight nubs trailing through her body to fire her core. She rubbed her breasts in an attempt to stop the throbbing. The sensation felt so wonderful she trailed a hand down her belly, slipping under the elastic waistband of her shorts to press on her aching clit. Desire wrapped around her like a cloud on the mountaintop and she was powerless to stop it.

Curses sounded from the deck above her and she startled, suddenly realizing she was fondling herself where Matt could walk in at any time. Heat flushed her face and she hurried to deal with the now-singing kettle. Her heart thumped in her throat and her hands shook as she poured the water into the French press she'd found. Then she leaned her forehead on the cool glass of the small round window in the saloon, trying to calm her soul. By the time the coffee was ready she was back to being agitated instead of direly horny. She stirred an extra spoonful of sugar into her travel mug in the hopes the calories would help her deal with the stress.

She stared at the second cup in frustration. She didn't

know how he liked his coffee and she was scared to death to go up the four steps to the wheelhouse and ask him. That would require actually looking at his face. Speaking to him.

Oh hell, she was screwed big-time.

The engine sound faded and she turned in a panic to face the door, her hands clutching her cup protectively in front of her like a shield. Solid footsteps paced away for a minute, a loud splash sounded, and then the steps returned. The door opened smoothly and his sandaled feet appeared as he took the stairs toward her two at a time. He stopped at the base, his chest heaving. His nostrils flared as he glared at her with his cobalt eyes.

He slowed his approach. One step. Two. The third put him toe to toe with her and she shrank back against the counter. He loosened her death grip on the cup, reaching past her to place it somewhere behind her. Their torsos touched and scalding heat flashed. Laurin realized she held her breath and she released it slowly, a puff at a time. He shifted and his firm chest brushed her already erect nipples. He caged her, one arm on either side of her body before deliberately pressing his hips into her. Oh hell, his erection felt huge against her belly. Moisture flooded her passage and she whimpered.

Matt leaned into her harder, every inch of their bodies in contact. He tilted his head and approached her mouth. She was sure he must hear the roaring beat of her heart. He touched their lips together, his eyelashes brushing hers like a butterfly's kiss and she exhaled with a little moan.

She was on fire. This wasn't what she'd expected.

Matt spoke against her lips, his voice shaking. Every word punctuated with a soft kiss. "You're...driving...me...insane."

Then the storm broke between them and his gentleness vanished. She flung her arms around him and pulled his lips to hers. Lightning flared between their souls, the frenzy of her needs whipping like the whitecaps outside on the ocean. He thrust his tongue into her mouth and she accepted it, sucking it in uneven pulses. Their hips ground together and she wrapped a leg around his hip, opening her body in an attempt to line up her clit with the tempting rock of his erection. He thrust into her, lifting her hips slightly to help and then it was there. Just what she needed—the angle, the pressure. She groaned into his mouth and he swallowed the sound. The air around them heated, rippling with magic as he lifted her to the surface of the counter. Behind her the coffee mug tipped, rolling harmlessly into the sink with a clatter. His hands were busy, unsnapping her shorts, tugging at her T-shirt.

"I need to touch you. I need to see you." He growled and stepped back, shaking his head like a wild beast. The lightning came from his eyes and she stared in fascination as he leaned on the wall across from her. They were all of three feet apart and it seemed like a mile. "I don't understand this. I will stop if you ask me to, but God I hope you feel like I do. I have to have you again."

Panic hit. Then delight. Fear followed rapidly by desire. His need poured over her, echoed by her own arousal. *Now? Here?* "The storm..."

"The ship is anchored in a bay. We're as safe as we're going to get." His hands clenched into fists, his entire body rigid. A wave of magic floated past her again, overwhelming her senses. She reached deep to try to counter it. It had been so long since she'd used that part of her nature her skin burned. The answering flash of passion that exploded from within was not what she expected. Instead of cooling her ardor for the shaman watching her with lust in his eyes, her fascination grew.

He was willing to stop? Oh God, if he stopped she would die.

Chapter Four

He waited impatiently, uneven breaths racking his body. Her eyes were huge—giant pools of midnight to step into and drown in delightful passions. He didn't understand the attraction between them, but it was innately right. At the very least, there was nothing wrong with them both enjoying another round of exceptional sex.

She nibbled on her lower lip for a moment. His heart skipped a beat as she answered him wordlessly. With a sultry smile, she shimmied her T-shirt over her head, reaching behind her to slip the clasp on her bra. She tossed the items in his direction, but his arms were too heavy to react fast enough. Laurin laughed as her clothing hit his abdomen and fell in a heap at his feet. He stared unblinking at her, his vision suddenly too full. Long slim legs, tapered waist. Her breasts were full and firm, red areolas crowning the gentle curves.

"You are so beautiful." He swallowed hard, unable to tear his gaze away.

"Your turn. I want to see your body as well." She slid off the counter and reached for him. He held out a hand to stop her. Any contact right now and he'd be embarrassed before they even started. He removed his shirt and she whistled approval, a sweet smile teasing the corner of her mouth. He longed to kiss the spot and inched closer. They met in the center of the small space, the heat of their skin touching before the actual moment of physical contact came.

Slow needy kisses followed, their mouths and hands and torsos meeting. There was no turning back, no stopping where this would ultimately take them. Matt thrilled at the taste of her, the sensation of her hands as she stroked his ribs. Her caress stayed firm and controlled, a fingertip flicking his nipple, trailing through the dusting of hair on his abdomen. He lifted his hands to cup her breasts and her sigh of satisfaction made his toes curl.

They stood for a long time, touching, caressing. Wrapping around each other, their bodies and souls melting together. Slowly it became too much to wait, his need making him hot and hard and aching.

When she dropped to her knees before him he swore the walls vibrated with the pulse of adrenaline that drove through him. The light kisses she planted on his belly taunted him, his cock tightening impossibly against the khaki fabric of his shorts. She slipped his button free and maneuvered open the zipper, his cock so sensitized she could have been brushing his skin. When she took his erection into her hand, he thought he'd die with the pleasure of it. The confident way she stroked him made a streak of jealousy rise at anyone else she'd ever touched.

"I want to taste you." The way her big eyes shone as she stared at him made his knees weak. She lapped the sensitive slit, cleaning off the bead of precome that pearled there, and he trembled.

"Yes. Oh God, yes. No wait...we need to talk." The boat rocked from side to side in the rising ocean, and this wasn't the time or place. Whatever magic drove them—the timing couldn't have been worse.

She kept eye contact as she licked a circle around the crown of his cock. "Talk later." Then she wet her lips and sucked him in. The moist cavern of her mouth enfolded him, enticed him. He slid his fingers into her hair, the soft texture rubbing his palms like a fountain of silk. She rocked slowly, and each brush of her lips, each stroke of her tongue drove his need higher until he had nothing left but arousal and fire. Still she moved over him, sucking with dark pressure on each withdrawal. When she lifted a hand to fondle his balls, he held on to his control with a fine thread.

"I'm close. If you don't want me coming in your mouth, you've got to stop."

She wiggled below him, winking one eye before swallowing his cock to the back of her throat. It was the most glorious sight, her mouth spread wide around him, lips glistening with saliva and the tracings of his seed. She tilted her head slightly, adjusting her angle and his shaft slipped in a little deeper. Then she swallowed and a buzzing started in his ears. A low, persistent pressure that built to volcanic levels. And when she clasped his hand and locked his fingers in her hair, motioning for him to take control back, he lost it.

He cradled her head gently, but firmly, rocking his hips with increasing speed as she groaned and adjusted her body. She cupped her breasts, pinching her nipples tight before reaching up to roll his sac in her fingers. She hummed, and his release detonated. He held her still, his groin pressed tight to her lips as she swallowed and moaned, suckling his cock as his seed shot down her accepting throat.

His vision blurred, his heart raced. He'd never come so hard or long before in his life. She nuzzled her nose into the tender crease between his thigh and groin, then planted a final kiss on his abdomen. Matt stepped out of his shorts and scooped her into his arms. They stood there, wrapped together, breaths mingling. She buried her face in the hollow of his neck and purred with delight. There was barely enough room to move in the tiny galley as he rotated and opened the small door to the sleeping berth with his hip.

"Your turn, Moonshine."

His large bed was tucked tight under the foredeck, the mattress filling the awkward vee-shaped berth to its best advantage. He lowered her tenderly, brushing a strand of her hair back from her forehead. His skin tingled where they touched, and he reached out with his shaman magic, trying to come up with an explanation for the emotion and passion that drove him. Drove them both. She caught his hand in hers and brought it to her mouth, kissing and nibbling on his knuckles. Her pink tongue teased him, slipping between each digit in turn. The contrast between the teasing touch and the desire it stimulated shocked him.

He laughed and stole his hand back to remove her shorts, the pale yellow shimmer of her silky panties evoking an instant reaction. In spite of just having come, his cock filled again as he stroked a finger down the center of the damp fabric.

She shivered.

He smiled and repeated the caress, sliding under the edge of her panties and pulling them from her body. He was going to enjoy this as much as she would.

"I need to touch you, Laurin. I need to taste you." The boat rocked violently and she pulled him to the relative stability of the mattress.

He licked his way down her body, kissing her ribs, planting butterfly kisses on her soft belly. Every taste, every touch built his anticipation until with a sigh he settled between her thighs. He couldn't wait to take her over the edge again. Without warning, without build-up, he lowered his mouth to cover her moist core. Laurin arched into his touch as he buried his tongue in her body.

The storm faded from his hearing as he feasted on her, the sounds of delight from her mouth rising above the cry of the wind around the mast and, the slap of the water into the windows. The roar of fire through his veins was all he felt, the pounding of his blood in his ears all he heard. And her. Throaty moans, sharp gasps, delicate pants—all pushing him to make her pleasure peak cataclysmic. And when she called his name, her fingers laced through his hair, hips raised to him, his satisfaction matched hers.

The dire need to be all she wanted swelled in his mind. He pulled away to see her melted into the mattress, boneless and relaxed. The smile on her face as she reached for him seared his soul.

How was it possible that in less than a day's time his heart ached at the thought of leaving her? Was it possible the magic even now filling the small stateroom was the result of something deeper than their attraction? He ran a hand up her torso until he cupped her face. She turned and planted a kiss on his palm.

"Are you ready for more?" she whispered. The taunting touch of her hands on his back made him shiver. When she grabbed his ass cheeks and squeezed, his cock jerked in reaction. Her aggressive, take-charge approach made him grin, the sensation of her wiggling under him sublime. She lined them up intimately and tugged on his hips to pull them together.

Oh crap. "Wait. Condom."

Her eyes widened and she swore softly. He chuckled as he splayed across her, heated skin to heated skin, and reached with one hand to dig in the small cupboard beside the bed. This time she had forgotten. It was good to know he made her lose control as well...

A cracking noise followed by a resounding twang rang out, loud even through the storm, and the boat shifted violently, tumbling them both across the mattress.

Fuck. What now? "Stay here. I'll check it out. No use us both getting soaked." He dropped a kiss on her cheek and crawled off the bed to make his way to the deck.

The darkness of the sky obscured his vision, the rain and the wind competing in turns as they struck the sides of the boat. The edge of one of the sails had become untied and flapped like a rabid ghost intent on mischief.

Over in the corner he saw the splintered remains of a tie-down. The anchor rope had torn clean away, and *Stormchild* now moved under the propulsion of the waves and wind. Even as he rushed to the helm to manhandle the boat, an exposed sandbar rapidly approached. They'd be stuck until the storm passed and the tide turned. Who knew at what angle the boat would end up before the night was over.

They had to get away before it grew too dangerous with the rapidly changing depth of the bay beneath them. Leaving the steering to the sea's whim, he grasped the walls of the saloon for support as he made his way back to the berth. Chilled water droplets clung to his bare skin and he shook his hair out of his eyes. It was a pity they would have to leave the ship, but with a little luck they'd be able to return in the morning and continue their journey.

Laurin stood at the door, her hands shaking on his skin when he drew their bodies together. "Are we safe?"

The tremble in her voice made him pause, and he stroked her cheek in reassurance. Passion flared between them again in spite of the situation, and he smiled at the ridiculous timing. "The ship should be fine, but right now we have to shift. We'll wait out the storm in the water. Or we can swim to land and take cover there. When I found this bay I noticed there's a couple of small cabins marked on the map."

As he spoke she stiffened in his embrace.

He smoothed back the strands of hair that fell across her cheek. "It's okay. I can help you." If they'd had more time he'd have taken this step slower, but the storm forced his hand. A faint scratching sound dragged along the hull as the underside of the ship touched sand.

She shook her head and pulled away. Losing the touch of her against his skin physically hurt. "Laurin, what's wrong?"

The rocking grew worse and she muffled a shriek. As she stared at him, her pupils were small dark pinpricks of fear. "I can't shift. I need to... I need..." Panic rolled off her and he stepped closer, attempting to reassure her. The craft jolted and they both fell to the mattress. Laurin clawed at the sheets, her breaths coming so rapidly he feared she was having a panic attack.

He pressed her to the mattress, trapping her body with his own. They both panted, him from attempting to slow the unreasonable need surging through him to take her again. He forced his libido down, cursing whatever strange affliction affected his mind and body.

This wasn't the time.

"I can help you. I'm a shaman. I can shift into any of the People of the Sea. No matter what form you are, I can guide you. Even if you've never done a shift." The trembling in her body slowed. He stroked a hand over her ribs, sending calming thoughts, reassuring. He had to make her understand his powers were enough to break through whatever trouble she'd experienced in the past. He opened his shaman talent and poured it into her, sharing his desire to help her while he searched for her animal spirit.

"No!"

A blast of magic exploded between them, flinging him to the floor. Somehow she'd thrown him off and now scrambled away, out the door and through the galley onto the storm-lashed deck.

"Laurin!" He chased after her, both of them naked, both instantly soaking wet, between the pounding rain and the whitecaps breaking around them. Standing in the open doorway, he peered through the plummeting torrent. Ribbons of water descended around them in a curtain. "Tell me what's wrong," he shouted. "I can help you."

She clung to the railing. Her body jerked, tossed by the wind and violent tilts of the vessel between the rockers of the largest waves. Resignation passed over her face as she looked into the sky, water streaming off her. "Damn it, I really don't want to shift and I can't swim."

"What? Of course you can. I'll help you and we can swim together." He reached for her, scrambling along the slick decking. The ship creaked on the sandbar, lurching to the side as the waves smashed the craft. He stumbled and barely caught the railing beside her in time. "We have to leave now. Please, Laurin, jump with me. I promise I won't leave you."

She threw back her head and, to his surprise, laughed. Sheer and utter delight broke from her lips. The burst of joyful sound cut through the violence of the storm and made his heart ache with concern. Had fear pushed her over the edge?

She shook her head, her eyes bright as she gave him a wry smile. "You won't leave me? Oh, Matt. Since it seems I have no choice in the matter... I might not be able to swim. But I *can* fly."

She threw herself over the railing and he scrambled to catch her, his fingers slipping off as she shimmered. A heartbeat later an osprey circled back toward the ship before gliding upward, away to safety above the storm.

Chapter Five

Laurin skimmed the water's surface where she'd last seen the dolphin rise. She headed for the nearby shore, back-winging inches above the sand before resuming her human form. The wind lessened here in the lee of the hillside, but the night air and the rain chilled her naked skin. She wrapped her arms around her torso to fight the cold.

Staring over the ocean, she wondered how Matt would respond to her being an air shifter. The sound of his cry as she'd leapt into the air reverberated in her head—he hadn't wanted her to go. The temptation to stay wrapped in his arms puzzled her, almost as much as the need she felt to physically join with him.

She'd never needed someone this desperately before in her life. Her whole body itched to have him back. She wanted to hear his gentle laugh, and to feel again the way he stroked his knuckles over her skin. Oh damn, what was the matter with her? Less than twenty-four hours had passed and she ached to be in his presence.

Her rain-soaked hair hung in tangled ropes over her face, water pouring in rivulets down her back. A deep sense of peace warmed her heart as his head broke the surface of the water.

Long firm strides brought him quickly to her side. His naked skin glowed in the pale moonlight that snuck through a short break in the clouds. Around them the storm raged in gusts, whipping her hair around her head. She lifted her hands to clutch it back and he took advantage of the moment to step closer, pressing their bodies together.

"Air shifter."

She smiled into his twinkling eyes. "Shaman."

A shiver traced her skin. He wrapped himself around her, their lips meeting, tongues tangling. Heat built between them, driving the night away. Their skin, slick with the rain and the ocean's salt water, slid together easily as he lifted her into his embrace. She wrapped her legs around his waist, her arms over his shoulders, mouths never separating.

Need swept through her, her breasts tingling where they pressed tightly against his firm chest. She linked her fingers into his hair and tugged until he released her lips. They both sucked in air.

"Damn it, I am so paddling your ass for not telling me sooner," he growled.

Laurin's heart skipped a beat at the erotic pictures that flashed through her mind. A tingling sensation settled heavily between her legs and she ground her crotch on his rock-hard abdomen. Matt groaned and dropped his head on her shoulder for a second. He took a deep breath then spoke, barely audible above the crash of the waves on the shore. "You've got to stop. I don't know how or why, but for the last five hours I've fucking seen everything you imagine doing sexually with me."

The heat pulsing in her veins egged her on. "I'd think you'd love it."

He broke into a laugh and cradled her against his body. Quick steps carried them toward the tree line. "Hell yeah, but it's making this whole situation even harder to figure out. Come on. Let's find shelter."

He cracked open the lid on another plastic storage bin. "Jackpot. Dry off and I'll get the fire going." A clean blanket settled around her shoulders, soft and warm, his hands massaging her gently for a moment before he winked and turned away.

The tidy little cabin had been unlocked when they found it. A small wood-burning stove nestled in one corner, a table with one chair next to it. The single bedframe was attached to the wall, its mattress rolled and standing upright in the corner to protect it from mice. Laurin scrubbed at her skin vigorously, trying to rid herself of the lingering chill. After toweling off her hair, she wrapped the grey blanket around her like a sarong and joined Matt where he squatted by the open stove.

"Here, I'll take over. You need to dry off as well." They brushed shoulders as they switched positions. Laurin resisted the urge to lean into him, the heat of his body drawing her like a magnet.

"Coffee?"

Even the sound of the word made her mouth water. "Oh Lord, yes. Are you sure it's okay to use these supplies?"

Matt nodded. "You know the rules. We'll leave the cabin in as good a shape as we found it, and I'll restock whatever we consume as soon as possible. I'm sure we're not the first unexpected visitors here. The fishermen understand."

That was true. She'd had to shelter in a small trapper's cabin in the mountains before and never felt guilty. The kindling crackled before her and she fed a few more pieces of wood to the flames. Building heat reflected back at her and she sighed with relief.

She glanced at Matt. He'd dried off and found a pair of shorts in one of the totes. He grinned when he saw her watching him and held out a pile of fabric. "I don't mind what you're wearing now, but you might want a little more warmth."

They worked around each other in a companionable silence. Laurin pulled on the oversized shirt, its tails hanging low enough to touch her knees. Slowly the room warmed. The rain continued to beat on the roof, but now it sounded pleasurable, a part of the rhythm of the place. Rich coffee scents floated enticingly on the air, and she turned from where she'd been making the bed.

Matt gestured to the cup resting nearby. "I added extra sugar. Thought you might need it."

She wrinkled her nose and nodded slowly. "I guess I owe you an explanation."

He handed her the cup, then sat on the bed and carefully pulled her onto his lap. "Drink first. If you haven't shifted in a long time you need the calories."

Which warmed her more—the smooth liquid heat sliding down her throat? The heat passing from his body to hers where they touched? The caring tone in his husky voice? He ran a hand down her back, stroking and rubbing gently. She wanted to purr and nestle closer.

The emotions this man produced in her were incredible. Passion and lust and sweet longing for home, all wrapped together in a vibrating burst of life. Too much and not nearly enough.

She looked up at him. "Why do I feel like..."

"...you want to crawl into my skin? Spend the entire night wrapped together?" He brushed her chin with his knuckles. Stroked her jawline with his thumb. "I feel it too. An air shifter. I never dreamed of this happening." Their gazes meshed. The knowledge he saw her every desire made heat rise to her cheeks.

"Never dreamed of what happening? Getting trapped by the storm? I hope your boat is all right."

He shook his head. "*Stormchild* will be fine. We probably could have stayed onboard, only we'd have been sleeping on our heads with the tilt she'll hit before the tide turns. That's not what I meant. I can't believe I didn't realize you were from the air clans."

Laurin snuggled tighter into his body. It felt too right to fight anymore. "I didn't want anyone to know."

"Why keep it a mystery? Shifters get along, most of the time. No matter what species."

Laurin debated how much she needed to tell him. Her one-night stand had turned into something bigger. If she was honest, Matt attracted her immensely, but not only by the physical pull between them. The caring way he had behaved opened her tightly locked secrets. She wiggled off his lap to face him more easily.

"I left the mountains two years ago. There were too many power-hungry shifters trying to woo me to their side and frankly I got sick of the whole thing. Teaching is what I've longed to do, but they wouldn't let me alone. I applied for the traveling position, and I've been with the People of the Sea ever since. My family knows how to find me, but as long as I didn't shift the others were unable to track me down." She sighed and finished her coffee before placing the cup back on the table. "Now I'm going to have to figure out how to chase them off again. I bet by the time the storm clears we'll have a dozen of the more astute of the eagle and hawk clans winging their way here looking for a fight." Matthew's shocked expression made her laugh. "What?"

"Why would you have men from more than one clan type chasing you? You shifted into an osprey..."

Damn. "Well, about that. I'm kinda—"

"Holy shit, you're a shaman too." The light in his gaze burned too hot for her to maintain eye contact.

"No, hang on a second. I'm not what you are. In fact, I'm the exact opposite—I have no magical abilities on my own. Yeah, I can shift into any of the air clans. But that's the point. Since I can shift into anything, all the second sons and third cousins who hope to break into the upper hierarchies want me as a mate. I'll boost their powers."

Matthew's smile burst like a sunrise on a clear summer morning. "I think we're meant to be together."

"Oh God, not you too." The words escaped before she could seal her lips.

Confusion raced over his face. "What the hell are you talking about?"

"Look, just because I...we..." She stood, disappointment washing over her. She'd thought he would be different. She didn't want someone taking advantage of her innate skills, wanting her only for what she could bring to them. Before she could take a step he caged her, dragged her closer in one bold motion to rest on his chest as he lay back on the bed. Rolling quickly he pinned her beneath him. "Let me go," she demanded.

A raise of his brow answered. "You're being unreasonable. I want to talk and if this is the only way to get your attention—"

"The last time you tried to get my attention by flattening me you ended up on your ass." How dare he control her this way? She tried to ignore the small part inside reveling in the command he took over her. Mentally chastised herself for even thinking about enjoying his bossy behavior.

"Hmm, you really do like the idea of me paddling your ass, don't you? Laurin, listen. I'm not trying to take over your life. I'm offering you a solution to your problems, and mine." He nuzzled her neck and she shivered.

"Stop."

Matt chuckled. "Why?"

"I can't think when you do that."

"You're not supposed to be able to think when I do this." He laid a line of kisses along her collarbone, unbuttoning her shirt and exposing her torso to his gaze. "Fuck, woman, you make me lose all control." He pulled away and sat up, stroking her arm gently. "I need you, Laurin, but not to take over your life. I want you as well, and I think between the two of us we have the beginnings of a beautiful relationship. If you want to listen to my proposal."

Chapter Six

He nearly swallowed his tongue at his poor choice of words. The expression on her face returned to almost as panicked as she'd been back aboard the *Stormchild* before they'd abandoned ship. Shit, his brain had tangled in knots. He was never this stupid, never so undisciplined.

She was a bloody air shifter. Never in a million years would he have guessed she was from the mountains and not the sea. He felt so comfortable with her. So...right. *As if they belonged together.* He shook his head slightly and tried to clear the cobwebs from his brain.

"Relax, Moonshine, I'm not suggesting you and I get hitched. If what you say is true, there could be a mess of jerks looking for you on the morning wind. I'm a very convenient solution."

Laurin sat up on the bed and he worked diligently to ignore the fact her shirt gaped open, her sweet breasts peeking out from behind the fabric.

"What are you talking about?"

He shrugged, then let a ripple of his power fill the room. Her eyes widened for a moment and then she smiled back at him, mischief written on her face. "Oh hell, that would freak them out. You're like the big bad boogey-man compared to that lot." He wiggled his brows at her and she laughed. The sound died in midair. "Wait. What do you get out of the deal? Other than the fun of making a bunch of chicken hearts lose some feathers as they flap for the hills, scared to death?"

I get to take care of you. He wouldn't voice the thought. Not yet. But perhaps a little of the emotion driving through his veins, just a little, ran through hers. For now, he shared a part of his troubles.

"You know what kind of a family life shamans usually have?"

"Shamans don't have families. They..." Her face paled and she opened and closed her mouth a few times. "Oh my God, that's why you were surprised when I told you I wanted to use a condom that first time. Most women want to have sex with you so they..." She swore softly, shaking her head in sympathy.

He nodded. "They want to get pregnant and potentially have a powerful offspring. It's not an easy thing, to get pregnant with a shaman, but it happens. And, speaking personally? It's a fucking miserable way to grow up, with no father but some mystical presence who visits once in a blue moon. I have no issue with single moms, but the ones who deliberately set out to gain status through having a kid—their idea sucks. I'm not having it, Laurin. I want a real family some day. In the meantime, I've spent the past six months fighting off the women who simply want me to be a sperm donor. If I had you by my side, my problem would be solved."

Laurin nodded slowly, considering his words. She wrinkled her nose for a second. "I'm scheduled to teach at Bella Coola for a month. How long are you supposed to stay?"

"Two weeks. I could arrange to do short-term visits to some of the closer settlements on weekends when you're free to accompany me."

"I might be able to rearrange my schedule a bit. It could

work." Her dark eyes looked him over carefully. "What if while we're in this arrangement, you find someone you want to get to know better? I mean, you might miss out on the love of your life while we're pulling this charade."

I think I've already found her. Oh fuck. His gut twisted. *Think fast, Matt, she's not ready to hear that.* He forced himself to stay calm and relaxed. "I won't cheat on you if that's what you're asking. For now, I simply want a chance to relax and do my damn job. Let's give it a shot, and see what happens."

Laurin paused for a moment before she stuck out her hand and they shook, businesslike. Impersonal. A moment's guilt assaulted him along with the trickle of sexual electricity snapping between them. This arrangement would stand for now, but he had no intention of letting her go. At least this way he'd have the time to be able to convince her they belonged together.

The deliberate fluttering of her eyelids did strange things to his heart. Another erotic image flashed from her mind to his, and he clamped down on the groan of desire wanting to escape. She'd envisioned them naked and entwined, the pale light of sunset on their skin as they made love on the deck of *Stormchild*.

His heart beat faster as she slipped the oversized shirt off her shoulders. It pooled around her hips and he swallowed hard. His cock filled like a sail in a stiff breeze. "Laurin?"

"I figured if we're going to be a couple, we'd better practice. We need to be convincing for the boys when they arrive tomorrow. Don't you think?"

Oh God, she was going to kill him. Could a man die from his dick exploding? "Moonshine, I love the way your mind works, but I left my wallet on the ship. No protection. The cabin owners were prepared, but obviously not expecting mermaids to come waltzing in the door."

She crawled toward him, a sultry expression on her face. Passion in her eyes, her breasts swayed slightly as she approached and his breath caught in his throat. "You need to think this through logically. We don't need a condom. Air shifter, plus water shaman? Remember your science, medicine man."

His erection stood straighter and saluted with a hallelujah. "Shit, you're right." She couldn't get pregnant, not without some serious mumbo-jumbo first. Which he'd be very willing to go through once he'd convinced her this was more than a relationship of convenience.

Her fingers fumbled with the fastenings on his shorts as he tried to kiss her senseless. They rolled together on the tiny bed, the crackle of the fire meshing with the pounding of the rain. A symphony of nature providing a background to their lovemaking.

Their naked skin brushed as they exchanged wet kisses. Matthew took his time and explored every inch of her body again in the dim light of the cabin. Her gasping breaths as he nipped and suckled at the rosy peaks of her nipples made his body ache. Made his heart sing.

He stroked her gently, circling the rigid nub at the apex of her mound with his thumb, sliding his fingers into her wet passage. They kissed long and thoroughly. Tongues and teeth, heat and hearts. When she gasped out with her release, he captured the sound in his mouth, continuing to draw her over the edge until her whole body shook in reaction. Then he settled between her open thighs and nestled their bodies together.

Sweet heat, warm and enveloping, welcomed him in. He pressed smoothly until he was buried hilt deep. It was everything he'd ever wanted and still not enough. The urgent need for her—he'd thought it would diminish now they were connected intimately, skin to skin. Something was still missing. His soul ached.

He pulled back to stare into her eyes. "Laurin." His raging blood didn't cause the pulse within his body to beat out of rhythm. Something deeper, more elemental and wild was happening.

She cupped his cheek in a hand and narrowed her gaze, a frown creasing her forehead. "What's wrong?"

He shook his head. "Nothing's wrong, but I have to tell you...I have to show you." Unable to contain his power anymore, he let go of his restraint.

Bells rang in the small room, a deep tolling sound originating from his magic. Magic that tangled their limbs, stroked their minds. Laurin clutched his back, her legs wrapped around his hips. "Oh my God, what are you doing?" A shimmer, like the light of a million fireflies, lit even the farthest corners of the room. A breeze formed out of nowhere and brushed their naked skin.

"I can't stop." He thrust in again, slow and smooth, dragging his abdomen over her clit and tilting his hips to hit the exact angle he sensed she needed. Laurin sang out in delight and scratched his shoulders.

"I don't want...you to stop...oh mercy...yes."

Another thrust. Another. Laurin bit her lip and lifted into his motion. The magic in the room spiked and she swore.

And lost control of her own tightly reined power.

The supernatural essence of their souls—of air and water— met as they made love. The small cabin attempted to contain the elements within a twelve-by-twelve-square-foot space. There was hard aching physical need, the stroke of his cock deep into her body. The pull of her hands to bring their mouths together.

Her addictive taste, the meld of their now-sweating bodies and salty skin. All of it, oh so right and necessary.

And on yet another level they touched. Her thoughts brushed his mind, revealing the level of her excitement, as well as the longing for him in her body. In her life. He sensed everything—desires and needs—and he hungered to provide for her.

Her body tightened, the first pulses of her climax clutching him. He held on for another three strokes, trying to prolong her pleasure, before it grew too much to bear. Burying himself in her warmth, he let loose and emptied himself. His body joined with hers as close as possible.

Their minds and souls linked.

Images, emotions. Knowledge of her hidden hopes and fears rolled through him and he knew her intimately, inside and out. Her eyes widened and she cupped his face tenderly as his own history wrote itself into her memory.

Matt wasn't sure how long they remained, postcoital, still joined. He became aware he lay on his side, staring into her face. A single tear leaked from the corner of her eye and he kissed it away.

"What happened?" Laurin whispered, running her fingers through his hair again and again. "Did we do something wrong?"

He brushed his thumb over her trembling lower lip. "Something very right."

"We're...this isn't just a casual relationship, is it? We're something more."

He nodded, unable to stop kissing her. "You still have time. I won't push you for more than the commitment we made to help each other. But we complement each other. Not only in bed, but in our skills and personalities."

"The magic. I've never lost control like that before." She rolled on top of him, pressing up to straddle his waist. Her hair hung like a curtain over her shoulder and he reached to brush it back from her breast. The need to touch her undiminished.

"I don't think you lost control of it. You would have shifted."

She nodded slowly. Matt held his breath, waiting for her response. He knew what he'd experienced.

His world had changed.

Whatever happened from here on in, he needed her to be with him. But if it took more time for her to accept their joining, he had the patience. The People of the Sea were old in tradition. Calm and deep, able to wait until the time was right. He sat up and folded her in his arms. "I'm going to love getting to know you better. You still willing to take me on? Magical destinies and all?"

The wind rushed in where angels fear to tread. Laurin's voice was soft, but clear as she spoke. "You think I can ignore what just happened? I wasn't planning on making up wedding invitations, but that was a little more than sex we just shared."

She nuzzled against his throat and the knot in his belly loosened. The tension of the past months eased away. When she giggled, he pulled her back to stare into her dark eyes. "What?"

"You know how weird it is to look at you and know what you like to eat for breakfast? That you drive too fast and you secretly love to read—"

Matt laughed out loud as he pressed a hand over her lips. "That's cheating."

She kissed his fingers, the light shining in her eyes beautiful to see. "Not my fault."

He held her gently, his heart overflowing. "You don't know

everything, you know. We still have some secrets."

Laurin grinned at him. "Are you still planning on kicking the boys' butts when they arrive in the morning?"

He had to concentrate to answer her with the thrill racing through his body. "Oh hell, yeah. They even breathe at you funny and we'll have a new feather duvet for our bed on the *Stormchild.*"

The sound of her laughter intoxicated him and he reached for another shot of pure sweet Moonshine.

The rest? They'd figure out the details as they went along.

Stormy Seduction

Dedication

To my friend, Leah Braemel, who motivates me to keep moving forward as we do Flying Fingers word sprints in two different time zones. You make me smile, girl. Onward and upward.

Chapter One

So this was what it felt like to be in the eye of a hurricane.

The beach under her butt was still wet from the previous night's pounding rain. The storm that had driven them to this small, secluded island had finally broken in the wee hours of the morning and now the crisp promise of a new day surrounded her. Laurin Marshall tucked a loose strand of hair behind her ear, the cool breeze off the water brushing her skin like a caress.

The calm was deceptive and soon to be torn apart.

Out in the bay the sunrise turned the water to shimmering gold, framed by the distant mountains of the British Columbia coastline. Marring the tranquil scene were the bare white boards of the underside of the *Stormchild* as she lay tilted awkwardly, the single-masted yacht trapped on the sandbar they'd hit during the storm. A flash of anger rushed Laurin— being stranded like this was not what she'd expected. Not what she'd fought so long and hard for during the past two years. She picked up a stone from beside her bare feet and tossed it angrily at the ocean.

She'd made sacrifice after sacrifice, the greatest of which had been never shifting.

Laurin rose, wiping the sand from her palms against the dangling tails of the only garment she wore, the oversized shirt they'd found in the cabin where they'd sheltered for the night. She needed to move, needed to burn off some of the nervous energy racing through her veins.

It had felt incredible to be able to be herself again for one brief moment. Forced by the storm to abandon ship, Laurin had thrown herself into the wind and shifted into an osprey. The wind under her wings had been achingly good... She shivered at the memory. She hadn't wanted to change back.

She hadn't wanted *anything* to change, but it seemed that was all she was going to get. Damn it all. Laurin kicked at the sand in frustration, torn between crying and raging at the injustice of it all.

There are many things we don't ask for, but still receive.

She paused in mid-stomp, the words of her grandfather returning to her. That first time, when she'd surprised her whole clan, he'd looked at her so seriously. So kindly. Laurin snorted in bitter amusement. She'd been wavering between tears and shouting that day as well...

"This...you call this a gift? How can this be good, Grandfather?" Her limbs trembled from the aftereffects of her first flight. Her first time ever having turned into one of the giant birds of prey that the People of the Air could assume.

Only she was of the peregrine falcon clan, and she'd shifted into an eagle.

Grandfather sat back, waving away the rest of the people crowding around. Finally only her parents remained, her mother cradling her in her arms. Laurin turned her face into her mother and breathed deeply, smelling the familiar scents of home and happiness. Today was supposed to be a celebration, and instead there had been shouts of fear and confusion. Her ten-year-old heart and mind were overwhelmed.

Grandfather drew on his pipe. Slow and even. His measured and thought-out actions were unlike most of the People of the Air who tended toward impulsive and rash behavior. He pulled the end of the pipe from his mouth and pointed the end at her as he spoke. A rush of tobacco and incense swirled on the air, and his words wrapped around them like an entangling vine covering the mountainside.

"There are many things we don't ask for, but still receive." He motioned over the foothills that lay before them, gestured up to the snow-covered crags of the Rocky Mountains towering at their backs. "The sun rises and warms us. The earth and rivers provide food, and beauty to delight our eyes in the colors of her flowers and the richness of her grasses."

Laurin pulled away from her mother's comfort, propping her fists on her boyish hips. She was upset; she didn't want to hear about the bounty of the earth right now. "Grandfather, I changed into an *eagle*."

"So you did." He smiled at her and opened his arms. She crawled into his lap as if she were no more than a baby. "My child, the Great Spirit knows what he is about. Trust that there is a reason for this."

A reason for her to be different from all the other children? Not what she wanted to hear. The pleasure of the flight was the only thing keeping her from fully bursting into tears. "I don't want this, Grandfather."

"I know, but it is what you are. There will be good from this—I see it. The water wears down the mighty mountains, carving her destiny. The air carries the seed on the wind to a new home, bringing new life. You will be the one who brings balance, my child. It will test you, and shake you, but you are strong. You are *Hawáte*."

He kissed her nose, then settled into a gentle rocking

motion, humming a prayer song low under his breath. Laurin pressed her ear against his chest and listened to his heart beat, strong and steady. She would bring balance. Okay. Maybe it wouldn't be so bad after all...

Laurin blinked and shook herself. She'd resettled on the beach as she reminisced, seated cross-legged, her body rocking with the tempo of her Grandfather's tune. She deliberately finished the prayer song, rubbing the stone she discovered in her fingers. The smooth surface warmed under her touch and she swallowed hard.

She'd left her clan when it became clear that the only balance the men were interested in was the balance of power. Once she had grown to maturity, and it became common knowledge she could shift into any of the air shifter clans, the rumbles had begun. Especially when it was learned her ability as a *Hawáte* would enhance the power of her mate. Yet she had no intention of becoming a pawn in some kind of hierarchy battle amongst her people. A cooling breeze ruffled her hair and she looked out over the ocean.

Hiding only worked if she didn't shift, and last night she'd as good as sent out a beacon announcing her whereabouts. After two years of working as a traveling teacher, her cover was blown. There would be air shifters arriving sometime today, looking to claim her.

Prophecies and predestined omens were a pain in the butt.

The ship in the bay caught her eye again. The only bright spot she could think of was Matt. Tall, dark, infinitely droolworthy. Although she should probably consider the shaman of the People of the Sea, even in her thoughts, with a little more respect than *yummy*.

It was difficult to believe they were lovers. She'd spent two years hiding, and remaining celibate. The first man she'd broken her sexual fast with had not only rocked her world, they'd set off a magical backlash that seemed to indicate they were... Well she wasn't exactly sure what they were. Definitely something more than a one-night stand. Her cheeks flushed at the memory of crawling out of his bed the previous morning with the objective of never seeing him again. It hadn't worked. Their one night of bliss had been followed by a tangled web that had eventually led them here, to this island.

It seemed the Great Spirit was still playing games with her.

Suddenly she had to see him. Had to be with him. Wrapping her fist around the stone, she ran the thin path through the trees back to the rustic one-room fisherman's cabin.

Storm-freshened air surrounding her, Laurin slipped silently inside. She leaned against the door and watched enthralled as her lover stood after loading the small stove with wood. The embers caught rapidly, and golden light flickered off Matt's dark skin, the firm muscles of his legs and ass shifting smoothly as he wandered to the tiny sink to grab the solid tin coffeepot.

She licked her lips and hummed in appreciation. "There is something so sexy about a man's bare butt."

He twirled, stark naked, a happy smirk on his face. It was impossible to ignore the proof that his interest in her grew more and more by the second. "You were gone when I woke. I thought maybe you were going to try to skip out on me. Again."

She shook her head as she tore her gaze from his groin. "I'm sorry, I shouldn't have done that yesterday. One-night stands never have been my thing."

"And it wasn't this time either—a one-night stand, that is." Matt strode to her side and cupped her face in his hands. His voice softened, caressing her ears, smoothing her senses. "Good morning, Miss Marshall."

"Mr. Jentry." Laurin's heart rate sped up as he rubbed his thumb over her bottom lip. "Are you planning on getting dressed sometime soon?"

"Clothing optional, at least for now."

His lips brushed hers, fleeting, like a lingering gust of wind from the tempest that had chased them into this remote island cabin. She could hardly curse the storm—it had been the catalyst that had brought them together as more than simply lovers. Laurin pressed her mouth against his, longing to feel the fire that he'd awoken in her, the magic.

Matt leaned closer, his skin heating her through the fabric of her shirt. She wrapped her arms tight around his neck and melted, welcoming his touch, his kiss.

A loud *pop* rang out from the fire, interrupting their interlude. She had no idea how long they'd stood there, but somehow already the kettle whimpered and hissed, and they reluctantly separated.

Laurin nodded toward the stove. "I'll get that. I don't want you to splash anything...vital."

He laughed as she brushed his erection with her fingertips en route to the kettle. He was hard, his cock jutting out proudly, and she really couldn't care less about making coffee. Still, at some point, this day was going to change from carefree to one with an agenda.

It was difficult to believe how much her world had changed in less than two days. From being a simple traveling teacher amongst the People of the Sea to—she wasn't sure what she would be called now. She glanced at Matt. He stood beside the single bed they'd shared the night before and was making it up, his bare butt teasing her as it flexed.

"What are we?" she asked, attempting to ignore the streak of fire that shot through her. The temptation to touch him, to press him to the bed and crawl on top for more sexual delight overwhelmed her senses. Whatever magic they had loosed between them, a water shifter shaman and an air shifter, the residual effects were powerful and long lasting.

Matt sat on the mattress and considered her seriously, his dark hair falling across his brow in heavy contrast with the dazzling purity of the blue in his eyes. "I don't know if I understand the question. Are you asking if as part of a shaman couple you have a formal title? Or are you asking if we're married or..."

Laurin frowned as she replaced the kettle on the tiny countertop and put together cups of coffee for them both. "I know we're partners—we established that last night. We belong together and I have no issues with it. I just don't understand it completely."

He held out his hand for the cup she offered and settled her at his side. "I don't understand it completely either. As a shaman, the balance of nature directs me to healing and helping. My strong tie to the ocean comes from being a water shifter. As a trained physician, I see where a person's sickness is wrapped up with the ills of nature. Curses and blessings, disease and cures—they are simply different sides of the same coin."

The steaming hot coffee cleared the final morning fogginess as Matt spoke. Laurin curled her legs up and leaned on the back wall, her feet tucked under his hard thigh.

She couldn't resist touching him.

"I know your role as a shaman, or at least I know what the shaman from my clan, from the People of the Air, did. What I don't understand is why the two of us set off such an explosive reaction. Have you ever heard of an air shifter and a water shifter joining?"

Matt nodded slowly. "A few times. It's rare, partly because you air shifters, my beautiful woman, tend to stay in the mountains. Too far away for us poor ocean dwellers to witness your beauty and fall hopelessly in love."

She stilled. It was too soon to speak of love. She admired him, she wanted him. There was no denying there was something mystical to indicate they were meant to be together at least for a short while, but love?

Not after thirty-six hours. Not when there were other issues flapping their way toward the island.

He put his mug to the side and captured her free hand in his. "What are we? For now, accept that we are meant to be partners as we head to your next teaching assignment and my next medical tour. Beyond that, we will be there for each other as needs arise, and somewhere along the line I hope it will become clearer exactly what we *are*."

The doubts and fears she'd been wrestling with on the beach returned. "Well, I hate to be the bearer of bad news, but that *needs arising* thing is probably going to be fairly soon, at least on my part."

"Your pursuers?"

"Since the storm didn't break until nearly three in the morning, we might have until noon. But I wouldn't be surprised to see a group of men arriving as soon as they can get here." She stared at their linked hands. "I'm sorry for bringing trouble on you so quickly."

Matt lifted her fingers to his lips. "Now you're assuming I don't want to have a good fight to prove my affections for you are of the highest quality."

When she raised her head to stare into his eyes, she spoke

firmly, resolute. "I don't want you to get hurt."

He snorted in derision. "Are you forgetting I'm a shaman? I have more power available to me than second and third sons could ever dream of. Any lower-level opportunists from your people hoping to gain advancement using you will have to go through me."

As long as that was *only* who arrived. She needed to warn him, just in case. "There might be a few...higher-level males as well." He raised a brow and she hurried on. "I can shift into any of the air forms, remember?"

"As I can for the water people. Go on."

She hesitated. How much should she say? "There were a few clans—the golden eagles and the red-tailed hawks—that have twins as potential leaders. Only one brother can eventually take charge of the clan, and..."

The expression on his face calmed her fears a little more. He was furious on her behalf. "They were jostling to join with you for a power booster. Don't worry, I can handle them."

Mysteriously, her coffee mug disappeared and she found herself pressed back against the mattress. Matt loomed over her, his fingers circling the buttons on her shirtfront.

"You think the storm last night slowed them down? Since there's really nothing I can think of that needs to be done right now..." The fabric parted and his warm fingertips drew designs on her bare skin, his gaze fixed on her torso.

She swallowed hard. "The *Stormchild*. I saw her on the sandbar. Shouldn't we be seeing if we can get her afloat?"

Matt leaned over to lick a circle around one nipple and a great shiver of desire shook her. His voice was husky when he lifted high enough to hover over the tightly pebbled surface. "The tide is low. Nothing we can do...except wait."

He lowered his head and enveloped the aching tip with his mouth, hot and wet, and Laurin moaned in appreciation. Their lovemaking felt fresh, like the sparkling water droplets clinging to the grass outside the cabin. Matt plied his skills on her body, taking one breast, then the other, under his tongue. Teasing the sensitive tips to rock-hard points before brushing the back of his knuckles against the tender under curve.

He played her, working his hands down her body, kissing his way back up to her lips. The journey was slow, thorough, as he licked her collarbone, suckled on the pulse point in her throat. Traced intricate patterns with his tongue behind her ear before dipping into the hollow of her ear. The erotic sensation of his tongue mixed with the sheer wickedness of his finger's path. Over her belly, stroking through the curls of her mons. When his tongue delved into her ear, it was in time with the press of his fingers into her sex.

She moaned out his name, opening her legs wider to allow him better access. Her thigh pressed against his erection, moisture clinging to her skin where his seed brushed her.

Thirty-six hours and he already knew exactly where to touch her to drive her wild. Whether it was because they were destined to be partners, or because he was just that good a lover, Laurin really didn't care about the whys at this moment.

She rolled toward him and captured the back of his neck in her hand and forced their lips together. The whys could wait. Right now she needed to let the passion building between them find a path of release that would allow the tiny cabin to remain intact. The image of flames surrounding them as they made love filled her mind, flickers of heat licking up her spine as she pictured riding him hard.

Matt pulled back from her lips with a laugh. "We are going to have to experiment to discover why I see all your dirty dreams."

Oops. Although it was a fascinating discovery, there were other things on her mind. "I'd forgotten about that. Sure. Research. Later."

Strong hands gripped her and Laurin found herself straddling his thighs, solid muscle under her limbs. The firm length of his shaft was trapped upright between them as he dragged her tight against his torso.

"Let's try not to set any fires, but if you want to be on top, I'm all for it. Set the pace, my ray of moonshine." Matt nuzzled her neck and Laurin laughed.

Shaking with anticipation, she lifted her hips and reached down to guide him. The hard, hot tip of his cock nestled between the lips of her labia as she slowly, an inch at a time, accepted him into her body.

He dropped his head back and groaned aloud. "Sweet mercy, that feels incredible. So right. Oh God, Laurin, don't stop."

As if she would. She undulated over him, one deliberate movement after another, moisture gathering in her core as he pierced her deeper than she thought possible. The drive of his thick shaft into her sex made her pant with desire. She changed the tempo, mixing it up. First fast, then slowing to barely move over him until he broke.

He clasped her hips and stood. She threw her arms around his neck with a squeal. "I thought I got to set the pace."

Enormous dark pupils stared back at her as he jostled her, finding his balance. His cock imbedded in her body, her legs wrapped around his waist, he staggered two steps to press her against the nearest wall. "I lied. You're going too damn slow."

Laurin laughed in delight for all of a second before the air rushed from her lungs as he lifted her hips and drove her down hard. Again and again he plunged her onto his cock, stretching her with his width, the rigid length hitting sweet spots inside that made her quivering need expand out to encompass her entire body.

She tried to participate, but was unable to do much more than cling to him, her breasts bouncing against his chest on each thrust. The sounds of their moans and words of desire intertwined with the scent of their bodies, sex and masculine desire. Then the fire she'd seen in her imagination flamed to life and took hold of her. It began in her womb and spread outward to consume her. Matt grunted and angled his hips for one final thrust before shaking with his own release, heated semen flooding her passage as he came with a cry. She tightened her grasp, fighting to hold on as her vision fogged. Each breath seemed to sizzle, the cooler air around them catching fire as it entered her lungs, her body so heated by their exchange. It took a long time until there was nothing left but lingering sexual satisfaction and the flickering threads of the inferno slowly dying away.

They collapsed back to the bed, Laurin on top of Matt in a sweaty, satiated heap, and she realized while there were some things she didn't understand, she was more than content to face the future with him by her side. His fingers trailed down her back, intimate, tender. They lay together, pounding hearts slowing.

"I thought you said you couldn't work magic?" Matt exhaled hugely, contentment pouring from him as he continued to caress her skin.

She laughed. "I can't. I just enhance other's powers. *Hawáte*—it means one. I join with you and strengthen your abilities."

He pressed his lips to her temple delicately. "Hmm, I could

have sworn there was magic involved in what we just did."

The teasing answer she'd been about to make vanished as a piercing scream broke the stillness, carrying through the log walls. The haunting cry of a predatory bird at the hunt, and Laurin stiffened.

The air shifters seeking her had arrived, far earlier than expected.

Chapter Two

"Dress." Matt pointed to the shirt he'd recently stripped from Laurin's body. He waited to make sure she followed his directions before touching her cheek gently. As a shifter, nudity didn't bother him, but he was suddenly very possessive about anyone getting to see Laurin. Especially men who were interested in her for what she could provide, not because they cared about her.

He made his way to the window to check what was happening outside. A little forewarning was a good thing, even though his strengths as a shaman should be more than adequate for any challenge.

"So much for them showing up after noon," she complained, joining him at the window, her body pressed warm and soft against his back as she peered over his shoulder.

Matt slipped his arm around her waist, breathing in her scent, loving the way she instinctively nestled closer against him. "Now is better than fifteen minutes ago. I'm glad they didn't interrupt us."

A light kiss connected with his cheek. "I'm glad as well."

He took his time to consider and judge what to do. Waking to find Laurin missing had thrown him for a loop for a moment. The connection he felt for her was incredibly strong for knowing her such a short period, but until she caught up to his level of devotion, he would bide his time.

But waiting for her to grow to care for him didn't mean that the blood pounding through his veins was any less hot to administer justice upon her tormentors. No one should have to hide from their family or clan. No one should be able to affect another life that powerfully without their permission.

He reached deep to find peace, seeking the cool energies of the ocean to settle the fiery burn of the sun. High in the air a group of birds circled, riding the currents far above them. "They must have impressive wingspans for me to be able to see them at this distance."

Laurin snorted. "About the only thing impressive about most of them."

Matt led her to the door, and paused. One long, slow perusal over her revealed pretty much what he expected to see. Her blonde hair hung in a beautiful mess over her shoulders, her ruby lips were swollen from their kisses and her face still held the flush of her arousal. She looked as if she'd been ravished, and if that alone didn't set their visitors off with a challenge or two, the People of the Air had less balls than he expected.

He cleared his throat. One last thing to organize. "You need to promise me you'll let me handle this."

She frowned. "Me woman, you caveman? Matt, I hid the past couple of years because I felt it was the best option, one that would cause the least fighting among all my people. Since that choice is no longer viable, I'll do what needs to be done. And while I'm very grateful for you to be by my side, I am capable of helping you."

What excuse could he use that she would understand? "Of course you are, but this is my first encounter with the People of the Air since I officially became shaman. Other than you, of course. If I don't put in a strong showing, it could make my life more difficult down the road."

This was one of the first times to gauge exactly how powerful he could be when the need arose.

"Oh. That does make a difference." The tension in her body increased. "Matt, we don't need to—"

"Need to what? Prove you deserve to live your life as you choose?" She'd run for so long, she no longer realized her habit of hiding was stealing her joy. She deserved far better—and it was time she got to relax. Besides, everything in him called out to protect and care for her. She truly had slipped into his soul.

Laurin straightened and caught his hand. She paused, then spoke clearly. "I trust you."

The words were simple, but the look that accompanied them added volumes of meaning. Total acceptance, complete respect. She gave herself into his keeping, and the level of dedication that took humbled him.

"I won't let you down." He whispered the words against her cheek, holding her to his naked body for a second before leading them outside.

High overhead a dozen avian warriors circled, wings swept wide to catch the morning breezes off the water. A few circled lower as Matt and Laurin stepped out from the trees onto the sandy shore. Matt glanced over the water—his beloved *Stormchild* was still beached on the sandbar, but she looked to be intact. Once they dealt with Laurin's tormentors, they could turn their attention to the ship and get her underway again.

One minute the hawks and eagles were airborne, the next, five plummeted to the ground, shifting to human form to land with various degrees of ease. Matt noted the couple that made the change and landing look effortless. They were probably the most dangerous to deal with.

Laurin pointed her way around the circle forming before them. "Jessup from the Laird Range. Cody, once part of the Crowsnest Pass clan, until they kicked him out. Kilade of Assiniboine Mountain." Her voice trembled and he stepped closer to her side, their bodies touching at the hip. So, she had particular concerns about Kilade, did she?

The men facing them stared intently, taking note of his proximity to her, the intimate stance between them.

"Who are the others?" He gestured at the two she hadn't named on the ground and those remaining in the air. "Should we expect those still above to join us?"

Laurin shook her head. "They will only drop to rest. They must have decided they are too weak to challenge for me, considering who else has arrived. And I don't recognize the other two."

"You've drawn a nice crowd."

The disgusted expression on her face made him laugh. "I guess I should feel complimented so many men think I'm worth fighting for."

There was no way he could let that one pass. Ignoring the air shifters he turned Laurin in his arms and held her tight. "You are totally worth fighting for."

She flicked a glance at the challengers. "Umm, Matt? You know, if you weren't here, they'd fight amongst themselves. Last one standing would claim me, or at least try to. They don't know you, so you've become the focus. You just put a target on your back."

He raised a brow. "A target, hey? Shall we make it very clear that if any claiming is going to be done *you've* already selected the man you want?"

Matt turned his back to the others as if he considered them no threat at all, then scooped her up and kissed her senseless.

If he cheated and used a touch of his shaman magic simply to ensure no one jumped them from behind, screw it. He wanted to enjoy this moment.

Laurin was stiff and unresponsive for all of three seconds before threading her fingers into his hair and giving their kiss her undivided attention. Her tongue stroked his, the sweet taste of her mouth making him long for more than a quickie kiss. He cupped her butt, reaching under the tails of the shirt to caress the smooth bare skin. God, she was driving him insane. The cooling touch of her magic slid over his and he shuddered.

Pulling away from her was the toughest thing he'd done in a long time. She sighed, running her fingers down his cheek as she shook her head slowly. "I hope you know what you're doing."

She stepped back, retreating toward the ocean, adjusting the shirt to cover herself more adequately. Matt eyed her hungrily. "I'm in love with that shirt, you know. I think if I bent you over my arm I could—"

"Matt." Laurin took a quick peek at the others before returning his stare. "Stop it."

With one final wink in her direction, he slowly pivoted, reaching inside for the connections he had with nature to prepare him for what was to come.

The faces that greeted him were stern and fearsome. He smoothed his own features to give no outward sign of the emotion within his chest. The People of the Sea valued peace and tranquility, unlike the mountain clans who seemed to be far more open in revealing their angry passions.

"Welcome, brothers. I trust you've had a pleasant journey." He bowed slightly, giving the smallest token of respect possible. He was shaman here. This was his home territory, and his woman they had come hunting. Not that he'd word it that way in front of Laurin or she'd be likely to carve off his nuts with a spoon. Still, he would defend what was his.

The two unnamed arrivals stepped back, unease in their eyes. He stared them down as they retreated, a swell of pride flashing through him. Had they really imagined they could simply march in and take Laurin without a fight? If not with their own people, but with her? She was too strong for the likes of them.

The redhead Laurin had identified as Jessup stepped forward, his thin limbs bringing him within a few paces of Matt before he halted. The derision on his face as he looked Matt up and down was impressive for its arrogance.

"It was an interesting trip, but I long already to return to my family." He glanced past Matt, as if dismissing him as unimportant. "I am eager to escort you home, *Koldunya.* I have searched for you for a long time."

Sorceress? Even from ten paces behind him, Laurin's heavy sigh was audible. "Jessup, do the words *fuck off* mean absolutely nothing to you? I'm sure you've heard them often enough."

Matt kept his face blank but he wanted to rub his temples. Oh, yeah, she was doing a great job so far of letting him handle it. *Not.* Anger flared in Jessup's eyes at Laurin's words, and he moved toward her without regard for Matt. Being completely ignored was unexpected, but he'd take advantage of the opportunity. He reached out and grasped Jessup's wrist, twisting and dragging the man to his knees in one smooth motion.

Matt pressed the arm he'd captured higher. "I gave you a polite greeting, brother. Do I need to train you in etiquette?"

Jessup grunted in pain, unable to move without dislocating his shoulder or snapping his arm. He tossed back his head and

Vivian Arend

Matt snatched at his hair with his free hand, completely immobilizing the newcomer.

Matt watched the other two cautiously, gauging their response to his rapid takedown of one of their contemporaries.

The one Laurin had called Cody broke into a grin and laughed out loud. "I always thought you'd be an easy mark, Jessup. Accept your paddling and let the real men step forward."

Under his grip Jessup went slack and Matt readied for anything. Anything, except for Jessup to speak quietly. "I withdraw. Laurin is free from my attentions. I give my word and will leave the battle to others."

Matt remained frozen. It had been too simple.

Laurin called out to him. "Matt, let him go."

"You can, you know. I won't aid you, but I won't fight you either." Jessup sighed heavily. "I had to make the attempt. I hope you won't think poorly of me."

Matt eased his grip. He'd never fought with an air shifter before, and found this rapid and complete surrender very confusing—it took a lot to get water shifters to start fighting, but once they began, it didn't stop easily.

"She's enough to make anyone want her," Matt said.

He pulled Jessup to his feet, staying lightly on his toes in case of a double cross. Jessup eyed him with perplexity. "You do not fight like I expected. What clan are you from?"

Matt wanted that secret for a little longer. He told the truth, such as it was. "Clanless."

Jessup's brow rose. "You and Cody should have an enjoyable...discussion then."

He turned and bowed deeply to Laurin, shifting back into his hawk form as soon as he straightened. A few strong flaps brought him to a perch in a nearby Sitka Spruce.

One down, two to go. Matt faced the remaining challengers.

Cody directed a twisted leer at Laurin briefly as he cracked his knuckles, showboating his thick biceps. "I won't go down so easy," he warned.

Without another word he dove at Matt, slamming his shoulder into Matt's gut and taking him to the sand. Matt rolled, using the slight slope of the shoreline to his advantage, kicking hard to separate their bodies. Wet sand clung to their skin and Matt was suddenly very aware they were fighting in the nude.

Screw diplomacy. He had much better things to do with his balls than let them get smashed by some overgrown turkey vulture on a mate quest.

The beach was his turf, and he used the location to his advantage. A broken fragment of shell, a partially buried stick of driftwood to spear into an unsuspecting foot—Matt saw all the obstacles at a glance and planned his attack accordingly. A feint to the right let him throw a punch that connected hard with Cody's jaw. The man's head snapped back briefly as he roared out his displeasure, spitting blood from his mouth. Matt was unable to avoid the huge hamlike fist that slammed into his ribs in retaliation. *Goddamn.* Nothing broke, but his bones creaked in protest. Matt spun away, then darted back to land a duo of blows to Cody's face. Forget hitting the man's torso. If he hadn't seen Cody shift from a bird, he would have sworn the man was a bear.

Knowing how to fight on the sand helped, the uneven footing and sharp objects Matt led Cody toward aiding his fight. Yet for every couple of blows Matt landed, Cody got in at least a single hit. Matt saw stars after one, his vision blurring for a second. He was so concerned about remaining upright he almost missed it. A sliver of movement in his peripheral vision was all the warning he got, and he went to his knees.

Over his head a heavy branch whistled through the air to connect with Cody's temple. The beefy man didn't even sway, simply dropped like a rock to the ground as Matt backed to a safe distance to face the newcomer. The branch fell from Kilade's hand, a dirty grin on his face as he approached. "Hello, *hoga*. I think my brothers underestimated you."

Hoga? Matt circled cautiously. It was obvious there would be little honor used in this part of the battle. Keeping his gaze on his opponent, Matt sidestepped until he caught a glimpse of Laurin. She stood close to the water's edge.

"You have me at a disadvantage. Our clan tongues are different—what pet name do you give me?"

Kilade sneered, but remained silent.

From her safe position Laurin answered his query, "He called you a goldfish in Assiniboine."

A smile escaped. *Cocky bastard.* Matt dragged the back of his hand over his mouth and wiped away a trickle of blood. "I see you're getting your water shifters confused. Even the eagle treats the mighty orca with respect."

He moved, flashing to Kilade's side as the blows rained down. Elbows, knees, the heel of his hand—each struck a new location as Matt darted quickly in and out of the larger man's space. The mountain dweller's bulk moved slower than Matt's lean mass, but when he did land a strike it was enough to rock Matt's brain in his skull.

Anger threatened, gnawing at Matt's control. This man, and the others, had been responsible for Laurin having to hide for over two years. They deserved no mercy, wanting her only for personal advancement, using her ability to shift into any air form to increase their strength.

Still, he couldn't fight while enraged. He thought instead of Laurin's bravery, her willingness to share her talents with all the clans of his people. She deserved the right to make her own choices, and that realization gave strength to his limbs when he thought he could fight no longer.

After delivering a particularly hard series of punches, Matt stepped back, chest heaving, fighting for breath. In the background, Cody staggered to his feet, shifted, and unsteadily flapped his way into the tree to perch beside Jessup. Across from Matt, Kilade leaned heavily on his knees, torso bent low. Blood dripped from his knuckles, bruises and red splotches marring his torso.

"You do have a few moves," the air shifter admitted, admiration in his voice. "Shall we come to an agreement?"

Suspicion colored Matt's response. "What kind of agreement?"

Kilade straightened, one hand dropping to massage his kidneys. "Do you claim the witch girl?"

Matt snorted. *I wonder if Laurin likes her nickname as much as I like mine.* "Laurin? She and I belong together. The only agreement I will make is for that decision to remain as it is."

A grin broke across Kilade's face. "Done."

He held out a meaty hand and Matt hesitated. This was not possible. Damn air shifters... "Why would you fight, only to give up so quickly? Why challenge in the first place?"

"Perhaps I wanted to be sure she had a strong enough provider." The air shifter threw back his head and laughed out loud, the deep sound of his tainted mirth rolling back off the nearby trees with haunting echoes.

Matt let go his control and swept his mystical awareness over Kilade, seeking his motivation. What he found surprised him almost as much as the rapid conclusion to the fight. *Damn.*

The man wasn't lying. "You truly do want her to be with me."

The man raised his brow. "I am of the mountains, you are of the sea. There is no need for us to contest. She has made her choice, and I will abide by it, now that I know you are eager to keep her at your side, safe from all who would threaten her."

Kilade stepped back and turned to face Laurin. He bowed deeply. She deliberately turned away, refusing to accept his honor. Kilade snickered and spoke to Matt. "At the same time I hope you are strong enough to beat some respect into her."

Before Matt could retaliate for his insult, Kilade shimmered, shifting back into a huge golden eagle, his eight-foot-wide wingspan beating the air hard as he mounted into the sky. He circled over the beach once, twice. The third time he dipped his wings and headed back for the mainland and the British Columbia interior.

The others perched in the tree took to the air. Those still circling far overhead wheeled as one, and the whole mismatched flock of them followed behind Kilade's retreat.

Their rapid departure en masse left no time for anything other than a gasp of pain as Matt's own bruises made themselves known.

Laurin raced across the beach toward him, sand kicking up from her feet as she closed in. She skidded to a stop and shook her head sadly, her gaze darting over his face and torso. His lip throbbed as it swelled, vision in one eye diminishing.

"What am I going to do with you?"

Her touch was light, but he still winced as her fingers brushed a raw cut on his cheekbone.

She slipped back to the water's edge, stripping off her shirt as she went. When she returned, it was to press the ocean-soaked fabric against his aching eye. He leaned into her, using her strong body as a support under his arm. When she stroked

90

her fingers through his hair, he groaned. In spite of the pain in the rest of his body, the sensual touch was too powerful to ignore, especially with her naked body so near, and his cock woke up. A good fight always encouraged good hard follow-up sex.

Then she tangled his hair in her fingers and yanked his head back. Hard.

He squawked in pain. "Ouch, shit, what was that for?"

"You ass. I had to stand there like some helpless creature and watch you get pounded. I couldn't move for fear I would distract you at the wrong moment. Why didn't you simply use your powers?"

Matt laughed, drawing their lips together. He kissed her softly before staring into her eyes. Dark, mesmerizing. Inside them he saw her concern and the care she felt. It wasn't love, not yet, but it was enough of a start he would take it.

"Why didn't I simply flash them with my super shaman power?" He couldn't tell her that it would have been too effortless, and he needed to stake a bigger claim. On his territory, and yes, a bigger claim on her. She wouldn't understand the driving need in his veins to defend and make her completely his. He cupped the back of her neck and touched his mouth to her forehead. Satisfaction filled him as he smiled over her head, her warm naked body snuggled against his chest. "Let's just say there are times that a little honest physical threat goes a long way."

Chapter Three

The *Stormchild* rocked gently. Laurin hung onto the railing as Matt secured the anchor, and they were once again vertical and seaworthy.

"I can't believe there's not more damage to the ship." She ran her hand along a bulkhead, admiring the woodwork. After having spent almost twenty-four hours tilted on her side on a sandbar, the single-masted yacht appeared relatively unscathed.

Matt glanced around, a proprietary smile on his face. "She's a sweetheart. Strong and beautiful, all clean lines and sensual curves."

Laurin found herself at his side. "Hmm, I think I feel jealous of your former love."

His brow went up. "Oh, no. I'm sorry to have tell you there's nothing former about my love affair with my ship."

He danced out of reach as she swung at him, their laughter carrying on the breeze. She chased him good-naturedly, darting out her hands to tickle and tease. When they reached the wheelhouse he twirled and captured her in his arms, pressing her against him tightly.

He'd shifted to return to the ship, and the change into a dolphin had healed the wounds he'd gained in the fight. She ran her fingers over his torso, appreciating the softness of his skin over the firm muscles, the individual bundles flexing and stretching as he explored her body as well. The expression in his bright blue eyes made her breath hitch. Then he lowered his head and took her lips with his.

The kiss was soft, a blessing of his mouth against hers, his fingers tugging through her hair to allow him deeper access, his tongue dancing across the roof of her mouth. A moan of desire escaped her, the need for him to touch her growing by the second. Her breasts felt full and heavy, an aching emptiness between her legs.

It might be sexist, but watching him battle earlier, fighting on her behalf, had really turned her on.

He stroked her cheek. "We can set sail in the morning, and still make it to Bella Coola by dinner on Saturday. Does that give you enough time to prepare for teaching this coming week?"

She thought quickly. "All of Sunday to finish the final adjustments to my lesson plans? Fine by me. Will you be okay for setting up for visits?"

"Easily. Someone is arranging the general drop-in clinic ahead of time. I won't see individual patients until midweek." Matt lowered his hand to cup her butt again like he had at the start of the fight. His fingers traced the edge of the bikini bottom she'd pulled on after flying over to the ship. He whispered against her lips, "Why'd you get dressed?"

"I didn't think you wanted me hanging out while we were getting the *Stormchild* underway."

He nodded his understanding even as his fingers massaged her butt cheeks. "Well, for what it's worth, rest assured I have no issues with you hanging out, ever, around me. No matter what we're doing."

Laurin popped open the button on his shorts. "Ditto. Well, I don't think I want you naked when you're treating patients."

He caught her hands in his and pressed her open palms against his rising cock. "You want to play *doctor* with me?"

The image that popped into her mind had nothing to do with him in a lab coat, but everything to do with an intimate encounter. Did he want to play? Maybe he could take her from behind, pressing her against the raised decking, the glowing sunset shimmering off their bodies. She lowered his zipper and released his cock, smoothing a stroke down the hard length. Capturing the fluid leaking from the tip on her thumb, she lifted her hand to her mouth and sucked it.

He watched her, mesmerized. Pupils dilating. Breath increasing in pace.

The salty taste of his seed splashed over her tongue and she remembered the feel of taking him in her mouth earlier, during their first trip on the *Stormchild*. Of him filling her, controlling her, and she groaned out with need. She'd loved every second of it.

"Damn it, Laurin." He dropped his head back and thrust into her fingers. "I can see what you're thinking."

What?

He hissed his pleasure out, cupping a hand around hers to tighten her grasp. Every rock of his groin forced his shaft through her fingers from tip to root. "It's not your hand I see. It's your mouth. I'm fucking your mouth and it's so hot and wet and tight. I'm dying here."

Laurin smiled. He had mentioned that yesterday, and this morning, that he saw her fantasies. She'd never heard of such a thing. Hmm, maybe this was something they should explore in more depth. A mischievous thought overtook her, and she pictured herself on her knees before him, breasts supported only by her bikini bra. Like watching a movie trailer, she zoomed in from a new angle, to see herself looking up, her tongue extending to touch the tip of his erection.

His body jerked at the moment of envisioned contact.

Under her fingers his cock was hot and hard. In her mind it glistened with her saliva as he plunged into her mouth repetitively. Matt groaned aloud, his head dropping to her shoulder, her hands encasing him.

"Oh God, it's not enough. I need..." His words faded away, his rhythmic thrusts breaking tempo.

His breathing grew frantic but she wasn't ready to stop. Her mind's view changed to her lying face down over the raised section in the forward area of the *Stormchild*. She mentally opened her legs wide, showing him touching her from behind, his cock pressing into her slick opening.

Matt lost it. He pulled her hands from his body and lifted her into the air.

"Matt!"

It was only a few steps later he dropped her to the decking, twirling her around and yanking her against his body. He dragged a hand down her torso, caressing her breasts before fitting between her legs to cup her mound. The very obvious, and very full, length of his erection fit between the cheeks of her ass as he ground against her.

"I need to be in you, Moonshine, not simply watch the pretty pictures." His fingers slipped to her hip, and he snapped the sides of her bikini with ease. The tatters of fabric fell to the ground. "No matter how incredible the pictures may be."

He forced her forward, her upper body coming in contact with the smooth wood of the cabin roof. One hand between her shoulder blades locked her in place. He used his knees to separate her legs farther. Then his cock rested at her entrance and she held her breath. He'd placed her in the same position she'd imagined moments before.

"Show me," Matt demanded.

The visual images returned, this time mixed with the very tactile additions of reality. Not only did she see herself bent over, ass in the air, ripe for his possession, she felt—everything. The solid wood under her torso as her body warmed it. The press of his hand on her back, the cooling breeze off the water dancing over her heated skin.

The exquisite pleasure of his shaft sliding into her sex.

Laurin closed her eyes to absorb the bliss invading her system. The ridged head of his erection pushed through the throbbing lips of her labia. He stretched her slowly, and completely. No escape, no quarter given. She attempted to picture some other kind of lovemaking...face to face, her on top...but this time he laughed.

"Oh no, you troublemaker. I think I've got your number. We're not going anywhere but here." He cupped her hips tighter, holding her firmly as he increased his drives into her willing body. Laurin called out in delight as an orgasm flashed—her passage clutching his cock. She hadn't expected to come this quickly and the electrifying release swept her entire body.

"This is so good, Matt. Feels so good."

"Oh, Moonshine, this is better than good." He found a way to get a hand underneath her, and his fingers pressed her clit in time with his thrusts. "Try awesome. Fabulous. Incredible."

Each word meant another plunge into her core, deep and demanding, and the tingling sensation that always accompanied her climaxes shot to the heights again. Laurin squirmed, trying to give back, squeezing tighter on his shaft, pressing into his groin as his balls slapped against her. Time paused until there was nothing but the physical sensation of being possessed. The sounds of their bodies joining created a wet and sensual counterpart to the sounds of the ship. The musical chimes of the wires against the mast, the flapping of a flag, the smack of the water against the sides.

When she cried out again in pleasure, he went as well. His seed splashed into her depths, hot and wet, his shaft jerking within. It was a long time later the hands clutching her hips eased, and he rubbed gently at the slightly bruised skin.

Endorphins raced through her body, her muscles limp. She opened her eyes to peer at him over her shoulder. The blissful expression on his face—she was sure it mirrored the one she wore.

"So...?" There was no way to miss the satisfaction in his tone.

Laurin laughed as he withdrew from her body and scooped her off the platform. "So?"

"Better than good?" He nuzzled at her temple as he carried her back the wheelhouse.

She stroked her hand down his face and let the contentment she felt be her answer.

The heavy mooring rope thudded onto the deck, followed by the landing of a dozen feet. Matt wiped his smile from his face. The otter clan did nothing without a full contingency of supporters. Even now he saw the official greeting committee waiting on the dock. The entire clan must have turned out.

"Matt!" A pair of arms wrapped themselves around his neck followed by hard slaps to his back. He twisted to look into the eyes of a close friend from his university days.

"James, you devil. What are you doing here?" Matt gave him a quick hug. James had switched tracks from medicine to pure science, and Matt hadn't seen him in months.

His friend grinned. "If I need to research algae, can't I at least do it in the comfort of my own clan's territory?"

Damn, it was good to see him again. Matt snorted. "I suppose. Personally, I think if you're going to study algae you should have your head examined."

James punched him good-naturedly in the shoulder. His gaze darted past Matt, and his eyes widened. He whistled softly. "Excuse me, mate. Angel needing assistance."

The other man snuck around him before Matt figured out what had caught his friend's attention. When he did turn, a string of curse words rose to his lips and he bit them back in rush. Laurin had gone below to grab her bag and had just appeared up the steps into the full sun of the late afternoon. Her blonde hair shone in the light like a halo, her pretty face and tidy dress drawing attention to her trim body and firm breasts.

Fuck.

The otter folk clambered around the ship deck, fastening the *Stormchild* to the pier, grabbing medical supplies from the cargo section, and generally snooping into everything. Through the chaos, all Matt saw was James hanging over Laurin like a lovesick sea cow.

He should have expected this to happen. Of all the clans, the otter folk were the most blatant in their sexual appetites. Not that any of the People of the Sea were shy, but the otters— they took the whole definition of sensual to new levels.

"Thank you, but no." Laurin twisted James away and pushed between his shoulder blades to direct him toward the pier.

"Troubles?" Matt called, fighting his way through the extra bodies on the deck to her side. It was hard to believe they'd been the only two on the ship ten minutes ago. It felt like forever since they been alone.

Especially when she turned and gave him that look—the one that said she had something very naughty in mind. He concentrated on keeping his body in control. He did *not* want to sport a massive hard-on when he met the greeting committee currently marching toward them. It could be too easily misconstrued, and he didn't need any immediate offers of "servicing" from one of the many willing volunteers.

A cool breeze floated past his mind—that light touch he was beginning to associate with Laurin's connection with him as a *Hawáte*. She winked, then smiled sweetly. Damn, he was going to paddle her butt. She knew what she was doing to him.

He cleared his throat and focused on the issue at hand— his friend, who was as close to a sexual bomb as anyone could possibly be. Matt stared pointedly at James. "Laurin? You having trouble with anything? Anyone?"

Even as she shook her head, she pushed James's hand off her shoulder. "No, no troubles in particular. Why would you ask?" She tugged James's fingers off her waist.

James pressed against her back and leered over her shoulder, not even attempting to hide the fact he was peeking down the front of her shirt. "I've missed you, sweet teacher. I'm longing for more advanced lessons than you gave me last time you visited."

More? What the hell had the bastard done with her? Matt shoved James away and tucked Laurin against his side. He glared hard, sending out all the warning signals he could. "There will be only lessons in pain if you try to seduce my woman."

James froze. "Really? She's with you?"

Matt nodded, thankful for once Laurin added nothing in

response. "Really."

The otter shifter held up a hand. "No worries then, mate." He paused for all of two seconds before his face brightened. "Of course, if you need a third, you know where to find me."

The man just didn't give up. Matt pulled Laurin toward the pier. She leaned closer to whisper in his ear. "Third? You've been doing kinky things I need to know about?"

Sweet Jesus. That was exactly the kind of question he wanted to avoid having to answer with a full formal greeting about to occur.

Although—this was the otter clan, and he had his suspicions about exactly how this greeting was about to run. Could she really not know what to expect? "I thought you said you'd visited here before."

She grinned. "Well, since you're aware James already propositioned me, you should know the answer to that one."

Any response he would have made was lost as the rest of the clan moved forward to greet them.

"Shaman. Be welcome here." The leader Willam held out his hand, shaking Matt's firmly before turning to face Laurin. "And teacher. You honor us with your renewed presence." The man clapped his hands and called out loud, "Come, give them greeting, then we can lead them to their quarters."

Matt opened his mouth to protest. To inform the clan of the change in the living arrangements—details like they would only need one sleeping room—when he found his mouth suddenly full...of tongue? *Damn it all.* He peeled the clinging woman off him as quickly and yet as carefully as he could, concerned Laurin would be upset over him being kissed by another female.

He needn't have worried. She couldn't see a thing, wrapped in a huge bear hug and being thoroughly kissed by Willam. Matt fought off other women's hands as he waited impatiently for Laurin to break free.

It seemed to take an extraordinarily long time.

She was rosy-cheeked when finally released, sucking for air as she touched the back of her hand to her mouth. Matt reached for her even as she strong-armed off the next man waiting his turn. She slipped to Matt's side, and he scrambled to speak the words needed to fix the situation.

Laurin beat him to it.

One arm flung around his shoulder, her body pressed intimately to his, she surveyed the crowd gathering before them, the gentle rise and fall of the ship continuing beneath their feet.

"We would like the cabin at the top of the rise. I enjoyed that location the last time I stayed with you." Her voice rang out strong, imperial. She slipped farther into his arms, somehow tugging his hand across her torso, cupping his palm intimately around her breast. He fought to control his body's instant response, but it was impossible. Especially when she lowered her lashes and glanced up at him flirtatiously. "We need a large enough bed. And it had better be sturdy."

Matt groaned as she slid her hand around his neck and sealed their mouths together. The contact was aggressive, intense. Far more intimate than the kiss the otter woman had stolen a moment before. When Laurin dragged her fingernails down his chest and nicked his nipple, his cock jerked, pressing against her belly. She moaned with approval, grinding their bodies together, making him hard as a rock.

The cool sensation he'd come to associate with her ability to enhance his skills wrapped around them both. He felt a sudden tug and from nowhere, his magic flared. Power poured forth, blazing with a frightening intensity. He stretched out his mental and spiritual hands to contain the outburst. He stretched out his literal hands to take control of Laurin and separate them. He gazed down at her dark eyes to see them filled with lust, and a fair bit of amusement.

Around them the usually rambunctious otter clan had fallen silent, everyone staring with astonishment. One by one, they lowered their gazes, respect apparent in their posture.

Even Willam paused. He nodded slowly, an inscrutable expression on his face. The staccato sound of his clap rang out again. "Arrange it as teacher has requested."

There were a few final glances of astonishment cast in their direction before a dozen of the clan hurried to follow their leader's orders.

Willam bowed low. "You honor us greatly. I trust your time with us will be...fruitful."

Matt bowed in return, wondering what exactly was going through the man's mind. Matt prepared to use his powers to check, but before he could, Willam disappeared, vanishing into the mass of clan members still surrounding them.

The crowds flowed around them, whispered words of respect echoing as they passed. Matt waited until they were relatively alone before tugging Laurin to face him. He couldn't be upset—it had been one solution, although not the one he would have selected himself.

"Why didn't you simply let me tell them we were together?"

She raised a brow. "By the time we'd have gotten a word in edgewise you'd have had to kiss your way through ninety percent of the clan. No way am I accepting other people's leftovers."

He snorted. She *had* visited this clan before.

She turned and led the way up the path, her hips shimmying in a way that heated his blood. He got lost staring at her butt, imagining all the things he could do to that firm ass when she paused and turned back, hands resting on her hips. She jutted out her chin, and something inside him melted a bit more. He had teased that the *Stormchild* was strong and beautiful, but his ship had nothing on his lover with her temper in full sail.

There was a challenge written on her face and in her eyes. "Besides, sometimes a little honest physical threat goes a long way."

Chapter Four

Laurin gave a groan as she straightened up from where she'd been hunched over her computer keyboard, leaning her head to the side to stretch the tight muscles of her neck. She'd been staring at the computer monitor for three hours straight, finishing the next set of lesson plans to distribute to her students who were scattered across the Pacific Inside Passage. They'd spent two weeks with the otter clan so far, and tonight it was time to put aside the work and take a breather.

Warm hands landed on her shoulders, brushing her hair aside, and she smiled. As Matt's lips touched her neck she reached up to stroke his fingers gently. "Hey. You finally escaped."

"I swear there are four times as many clan members as last time. I don't remember general clinic hours taking this long before. Ever."

She swung her chair around to face him. It was after eight p.m., and he'd been at the clinic since seven in the morning. There were crease marks at the side of his eyes from his exhaustion, and she wanted to wrap him up and soothe him. She'd been working all day as well, but teaching had its own built-in breaks. Building sandcastles with the elementary students to demonstrate different kinds of tactile strength was more amusing than physically taxing.

Matt held out his hand and she went into his arms willingly. They snuggled close, Matt burying his face against her neck and breathing deeply. "I don't know what I want more. Food, sleep or you."

She laughed. "Why don't we do all three, in that order?" She tugged him toward the door. "Come on, I've got our evening planned."

It had taken a few days to figure out who to bully to get things accomplished around camp. It took a special kind of bartering and bossing to not become overwhelmed by water shifters in the first place. The otters had no sense of ownership and few boundary lines. Her trunk full of clothing was finally off limits only because she'd laid down the law and had Matt loan her an enhanced lock.

They took the "share and share alike" motto a touch too far in this community. Especially when it came to Matt. She glanced at him briefly, not even trying to deny the proprietary feelings she experienced.

Laurin led Matt by the hand toward the beach, swinging past the communal kitchen and grabbing the basket she'd prepared earlier. It felt heavy enough, but she took a quick peek to ensure no one had absconded with any of their picnic supplies.

Matt took the basket from her, linking his fingers through hers. "You have been busy."

"I figured you'd have another late night. I used it to my advantage. You're free until noon tomorrow, right?"

"Unless there's an emergency, but things seem quiet."

"I'm done as well. The night is ours."

They exchanged smiles before she led him down the path. Time had been passing in a blur with both of them working like crazy. The relationship seemed to have helped them both settle

105

quickly into the community in some ways—although there were tough moments. If she was honest? She missed the intimacy of being alone with him on the *Stormchild*.

They walked in silence, the soothing repetition of the ocean washing the shoreline their only background music. Even though it was late, this far to the north the sun still hung above the horizon. It was more than hour away from disappearing into the waters of the Pacific Ocean that filled the Bella Coola inlet. Matt's soft chuckle broke the silence as they mounted the ridge and the cabana she'd had set up came into sight. The bright color of the fabric shone against the bleached white of the sand and the neutral tones of the rocky shoreline behind it.

"Laurin, you are a miracle worker."

"Wait until you see inside."

He dropped her fingers and ran, all his earlier tiredness seeming to disappear. She chased him, her laughter bursting out. Every step they'd taken away from the settlement had felt as if they'd cut restraining ropes. She'd never realized how much energy it took to live up to others' expectations—or others' expectations of who she didn't feel she truly was.

Matt pressed aside the fabric door and turned to face her. "Did I say miracle worker? I meant a magician. It's gorgeous. Oh my God, there's a bed." He dropped the basket on the small table at the back of the cabana before falling face first onto the mattress.

Laurin tossed herself beside him, brushing his hair back from his face. "You want to nap first? Or eat?"

He rolled, snatching her up to drape her limbs over his body. "Talk. Then sex. Then eat, then sex."

A yawn escaped him and Laurin giggled. "Or we could start with a nap."

He shook his head. "I had no idea this stop at Bella Coola

was going to be this insane. How have your students been doing?"

Laurin folded her arms on top of his chest and positioned herself more comfortably so she could look him in the eye as they spoke. "The teaching part is going great. Being partners with the shaman? I've never had so many questions I couldn't answer before. It's like they think since I'm with you, I know everything you know as well."

Concern etched his face. "Is it causing troubles? That's an issue I'd never imagined arising."

"It's not bad—if anything it's been humbling to realize there is so much I don't have the answers for."

He stroked a knuckle along her cheek tenderly. "If you need me to drop in or speak to anyone, you let me know."

Laurin resisted voicing the evil thought that flashed through her mind. She could imagine what the women of the community would think about that—him leaving his busy practice to help her with the children. They already thought she'd somehow managed to snatch up the moon. She'd be considered a true goddess to have the shaman at her beck and call.

She'd never been the type to gloat, but then she'd never had someone like Matt in her life before either.

"There's one question you can answer for me. What's your clan?"

He paused. "I don't have one. I'm shaman, and—"

"I know, you're a part of them all. I meant, where is your mother from?"

A huge sigh escaped him. "One of the dolphin clans from the far north. We're not really close."

Laurin leaned up to drop a quick kiss on his lips. "Sorry,

didn't mean to pry."

"No, no. It's okay. I need to go visit her again sometime. It was easier to avoid going back than to deal with how I feel about the whole child-of-the-shaman issue. Silly, really. I'm too old for those kind of avoidance games."

She laid her head back on his chest and tried to send soothing thoughts. Family. Even when everyone got along, dealing with them could take a toll. Laurin changed the topic as best she could. "What's happening in terms of you and your clinic? Are you nearly at the end of the rush?"

He nodded, his eyes closing as he continued to stroke her body and play with her hair. "And I have to say thank you— there are a whole lot less random females popping in to ask for full physicals in the hopes I'll take one look at their naked body and be unable to resist ravishing them right there on the examining table."

"Glad that my presence in your life is working as a decoy."

Laughter rang out, his face bright even as his eyes remained closed. "You minx. You know damn well it's not simply your presence. The fact you stood up in the communal kitchen the second day we were here and announced you'd skin any one who poached on your territory has a lot more to do with my lack of annoyances than simply your pretty smile."

Shit. A flush of embarrassment hit. She really had no idea what had come over her that day. "You heard about that? You hadn't said anything, so I thought..."

His body shook under her as he laughed. "I heard. In fact, I had to offer the same kind of threat at the bonfire after you left that night. The men were all so impressed with your grit and figured you must be some kind of hellion in bed."

A warm curl of excitement lit in her belly. He opened his eyes and she fell into the blue depths. "I can be a hellion, with the right person."

Somehow they maintained that eye contact as their clothing disappeared. Warm naked flesh covered her, wet kisses and long shiver-inducing brushes of his fingers followed. They moved easily together on the bed, giving and receiving pleasure. Soft sighs and little gasps for air escaped her throat, and she didn't even once try to send a dirty image into his mind. Everything she wanted to experience was right there, everything she needed to fly over the moon already at her fingertips.

A warm breeze fluttered the curtains of the cabana, and Matt stopped his exploration of her body to slide open the fabric on the ocean side. The setting sun had turned the sky to brilliant orange and pink, bands of radiant light streaking across the bed and shimmering over their skin. She pulled him back to her side, reveling in his touch, the caress of his tongue drawing lazy designs down her belly. The intimate stroke of his fingers, the rapid beat of his heart as he brought them together, and they joined. Fullness, heat, and over it all, the tenderness pouring out from his soul.

She wiggled, trying to escape. It was too quick, and she wanted to give to him first. Pleasure shot through her as he leaned in harder, his body pinning her to the bed and holding her trapped.

"Please, I want to—"

"No. This time I give to you." He kissed her cheek, his eyelashes fluttering against hers like a butterfly and she relaxed back.

How could she resist his touch? Each caress brought her higher and higher. Drove the pleasure in her core outward like the streaks of color highlighting their bodies. They lay in a pool of fading sunlight, sparks of stars bursting through the haze of darkness appearing at the edge of the visible sky. Her nipples throbbed in time with her sex, both heavy with anticipation as Matt caressed and primed her until there was nowhere to go but deep into pleasure. Rolling waves of it that crashed far louder than the ocean that surged meters away from them.

"Matt, oh God, yes."

She clutched his shoulders, clinging tight to him as he merged them again and again. The intensity of her orgasm made her vision grow dark, her body squeezing and clasping so hard she felt completely out of control. Laurin gasped for air, striving to stay alert, needing to ensure his release as well.

The sound of shattering rock from the nearby cliff echoed around them the same moment Matt stiffened, his body held rigid over hers. He pumped his hips in tiny pulses, as if trying to dig even deeper into her core. His whispered words were too quiet to hear, but his eyes spoke volumes.

Laurin tugged him on top of her, his body weight crushing her to the mattress for a moment before he rolled them to the side, still connected. They lay there for a long time, touching, staring. Kissing slowly then pulling back to stare again.

The connection between them might be somehow mystical, but Laurin had a sneaky suspicion that there was the possibility for more. First she had to decide if she could allow herself to fall in love with a shaman of the People of the Sea.

Laurin dropped a kiss against his chest before yawning and forcing herself to crawl out from under the covers. Even the best of getaways had to come to an end, and their time was rapidly approaching. The supper picnic had been consumed at midnight after they'd waded and washed in the ocean. They'd talked and laughed and spent the rest of the night waking each other and tangling the sheets until she felt totally used and achy in all the right spots this morning.

They had time for a quiet breakfast and not much else before they had to leave.

She stood and stretched, turning to sneak a little secret ogling of his naked body into her morning. Instead it was his gaze fixed on her that caught her, a worried frown marring his forehead.

"Why are you looking at me like that? Do I have something in my teeth?"

Matt sighed. "No, I'm just trying to figure out how to say this."

"Is something wrong?"

"If you're talking about last night? Oh hell, no. That was everything I could have asked for, and I'd kill for another couple days of you-and-me alone time."

Her thoughts, exactly. "Then why the frown?"

"There's something you need to know, but I don't want to shock you."

Now he was being silly. She reached for the bra and T-shirt that were draped over the back of the chair by their bed. Somewhere during their exertions last night, he must have found all their clothing—she didn't remember hanging them up.

"I'm pretty sure I'm a big girl now. You can spit it out, and if I need to have the vapors, I'll warn you, okay?"

Something hit her in the back of the head and she turned with a laugh, scooping up the pillow and flinging it back at him.

"Okay, if you think you're ready. Tomorrow is summer solstice."

He fell silent. Laurin waited, reaching behind her to fasten her bra. "And...is that it? I was aware of that fact, Matt. Teacher, remember?"

"Yeah, well, there's a party tomorrow night, and I'm not sure you should go."

Laurin rested her fists on her hips, shirt dangling from her hand. "Are you trying to tell me to stay home while you go out rabble-rousing? What, is it a guys-only macho thing?"

"No. Fertility ritual."

Oh, shit. Yeah, those could get out of hand. Still, she wasn't a baby. "I've seen it before. I'm sure we have something similar among the Air People."

Matt shook his head. "We're talking the otter clan. As long as you're prepared, I guess it will be all right. Just...don't nod your agreement to anything, okay?"

She poked her head through the fabric of her T-shirt to see him staring seriously at her. "What are you talking about? What am I not supposed to agree to?"

"To participate."

This conversation was going nowhere fast. Laurin stepped closer and leaned over him. "Matt, exactly what kind of ceremony are we talking about? I somehow don't think it involves gathering seeds and grasses and tossing them on the bonfire, does it?"

He sat up, swinging his legs over the edge of the bed. "There is a bonfire and seed, but not the type you're thinking of."

She sat next to him and grabbed his leg. "Spill."

"I'll have to."

What in the world? Laurin punched him in the arm. "Stop talking in code."

Matt dragged his fingers through his hair and sighed. "Look, if you weren't here I would've had the toughest time explaining why I shouldn't be an active participant. As it is, they will still expect me to spill seed."

Okaaaay...maybe the air clans *didn't* do this ritual. "Are you talking about sex? I mean, your semen? And if so, exactly how and where do they think your seed will spill?"

"I'll masturbate."

"In front of them?"

"Trust me, very few people will be watching me."

"What else would they be watching?"

"Sex."

The word stuttered from her lips. "Se-sex? In public? You can't be serious."

"Oh, you innocent woman." He caught her in his arms and wiggled her around until she rested in his lap. "I thought you'd stayed with this clan before?"

Holy shit, this got weirder and weirder. The sexy interlude they'd shared the night before had seemed daring—out in a cabana with the curtains open to the air. But unless they'd had some peeping Toms, she thought their sensual performance had been far enough down the beach to remain unwitnessed.

The otter folk were managing to surprise her after all, and a part inside her that longed for the typical privacy demonstrated by the People of the Air quivered—a little in disgust, and a little...with desire?

It was as if there was a wild child inside her wanting to escape. "I have stayed with the clan before, but I obviously give off much more innocent vibes than I thought. I mean, I've been propositioned dozens of times, but I've managed to avoid seeing any open-air sex." Matt tensed under her, and she hurried on, trying to reassure him. "And I've never accepted any of the individual offers, or wanted to."

"You will not be participating. In fact, I really think you

should stay back in our quarters." His voice dropped a level, now insistent and firm.

Bullshit. He could chalk it up to jealousy if he wanted to, but no way in hell was she agreeing to that.

"While you go jerk off in front of the crowd? Or get accosted by one of the women? 'Are you all alone, shaman? I insist you let me help you.'" She stuck out her lower lip in imitation of a few of his more persistent hangers-on, and he laughed.

"Fine, but you need to follow my instructions while we are there without question. Please, this is important to me. I really don't want this event to get carried away."

Her curiosity flittered higher. "Get real. You're planning on masturbating in public and figure no one will be watching you because there's going to be something else more interesting happening? Oh, right—public sex. How in the hell can you be worried about the event getting carried away? I can hardly wait."

Matt grinned sheepishly, right before he snagged her wrist and tugged hard enough she fell back on top of him. Their mouths met, and suddenly there was nothing on her agenda but the rumbling desire for him that never seemed to leave her and a streak of inquisitiveness that she'd have to wait to satisfy.

This fertility ritual sounded very interesting indeed.

Chapter Five

The knock on the door was expected, but came far earlier than he'd hoped. Laurin still wore the flimsy swath of fabric she claimed was a housecoat, but he considered nothing more than fabric foreplay—he got hard every time she pulled the damn thing on.

The otter clan leader stood on the other side of the threshold, bowing deeply before passing over a set of ritual outfits for them both. Matthew accepted the clothing and placed it on the table beside the door.

"Our thanks. We will be there at twilight."

Willam stared at Laurin's body as she drew alongside Matt at the door, and Matt held off blocking her from view by sheer willpower alone.

"You know, I would be very grateful if you would reconsider your decision. Such an important occasion would be made even more significant with both of you participating." His gaze lingered blatantly on Laurin's breasts and Matt's hands clenched into fists.

Laurin stepped forward, and Matt held his breath. If she misspoke...he couldn't let her get roped into this situation, but she'd proven her intelligence over the past weeks. He rested his hands on her hips and sent her positive thoughts.

"Willam, your community has been very gracious in caring

for our needs. As a visitor among many clans as I've traveled with my teaching, I have to say there is a special atmosphere here among the otter folk that I've not experienced anywhere else."

Matt hid his grin. Like the fact they were constantly trying to get into her pants? No, he was sure that didn't happen everywhere.

She continued, "We are merely visitors to your people. We would not dream of taking away an honor from them."

Willam lifted his chin. "They would gladly give it up if I asked."

"Ahh, but that is not what your clan needs. They need a strong, decisive leader, as you have demonstrated yourself to be by having selected the participants." Laurin shook her head and crossed her arms to finally cover her chest. "No, we are honored to witness. That is our rightful place."

"But—"

Laurin leaned over and kissed his cheek quickly before snatching up the clothing and retreating into the cabin. "Matt, I really will need your help getting into these garments. How *do* the People of the Sea dress without assistance? I've never seen such..."

Her voice faded away into low mutterings as she laid the items out on the bed. Matt faced Willam again, the leader's expression far too readable.

"Your woman is a handful," Willam rumbled in frustration.

She was. She'd also proved more than capable of taking care of herself. Matt was ashamed that he'd felt the situation would be too much for her to handle. It was another reminder that they were only in the first stages of getting to know each other, no matter how much his heart was drawn to her.

He stepped outside to join Willam on the stoop, closing the door behind him. "She is strong and independent—and correct. You are a good leader, Willam. Taking away a position of honor at the last minute from two of your people would do nothing to enhance your powers, and everything to taint the ceremony."

"But you are shaman."

"And as such, I am connected to all the clans, not only your own. You are the heart of your people—you must keep them strong."

Willam stilled, his weathered face back at peace. "I shall. Thank you, Shaman. I will see you in an hour."

He strode away, head held high, and Matt waited until he'd disappeared into the collection of huts. The best and only way to have appealed to the man—his leadership.

Matt slipped open the door and stared at Laurin. She twisted to face him, garments hanging from either hand.

"Was that okay?" She tossed the fabric back on the bed and joined him in the middle of the room.

"It was inspired." He lifted her chin and kissed her lips briefly. "I owe you an apology."

Laurin frowned. "Why?"

"Because I should have known you could handle the situation. I forget that you've not only traveled among my people, you're a teacher. You're educated, and intelligent, and courageous enough to have left your home to do what you felt was right." He dropped to his knees and kissed her stomach, burying his face against her momentarily. Breathing in her sweet scent eased away some of the nervousness that had flared at discovering Willam at the door. He raised his head until their eyes met. "I'm sorry for having doubted you."

"Matt. Stop it." She tugged on his shoulders. "Stand up."

117

He stayed put. "Will you forgive me?"

She pulled again. "Not when you're on your knees like that. You were worried. I understand."

He stared up at her face, sensing the connection between them that he couldn't completely comprehend. "I was still wrong to treat you as I did."

Laurin sighed, shaking her head in exasperation. She dropped to her knees and wrapped her arms around him. "People of the Air don't ask forgiveness like this. If they absolutely have to, they say *I was wrong*, and move on."

"We of the sea like to make a bigger deal about apologizing."

She grinned at him. "So I noticed. You do tend to do things in big ways, don't you?"

An image of what she would witness in a few hours flashed through his mind. "Bigger than you expect."

Her lips brushed gently against his cheek as she leaned in close enough to whisper in his ear. "You're forgiven. Now come and help me figure the silly costumes out. I have no idea what we're wearing."

Matt squeezed her tight before leading her to the bed and untangling the bits and pieces of the garments. When he finished placing them in two piles, Laurin bent over and peeked under the bed.

"What are you doing?" he asked.

She shook her head. "That can't be all of it. There's not enough material to cover anything of importance."

He raised a brow and waited.

"Oh shit. Okay, maybe I should stay in the room."

"Sorry, that option is no longer available." He tugged on the belt of her robe, running a finger down her torso as smooth skin appeared.

If they didn't have a deadline to meet, he would have had far more fun getting her dressed. As it was, he had to be satisfied with dropping hurried kisses on her nape as he helped tie the skimpy halter bra around her neck. He pressed a kiss to the smooth skin visible above the scant skirt hugging her hipbones before lifting his gaze to admire her barely covered body.

"If there's a strong wind I'm going to put on a show." Her voice had dropped lower, filled with lust, and he trailed his fingers up the inside of her leg to touch her naked body. The curls covering her sex were damp and he couldn't resist rubbing the apex of her mound. She moaned, her head falling back, and he steeled himself. Pulled his hand away. Slipped on his own scrap of fabric masquerading as a loincloth.

"We need to go." He ground the words out. They had to leave now, before he buried himself in her heat and they didn't move for days, let alone soon enough to make the ceremony.

None of his desire had faded by the time they reached the ceremonial stage. They were greeted in a surprisingly innocent manner for the otter folk, and led to the chairs of honor at one end of the raised dais. Across the circle from them Willam sat in state, his chair rising high above the fire pit and allowing all the adults filling the perimeter of the area a clear view of his magnificence.

The scent of pine smoke and incense carried on the air. Torches were lit one by one around them, the warm glow melding with the sun's fading light. Matt reached out again to stroke Laurin's braid, the heavy weight of her blonde hair woven tightly into a single tail hanging down her bare back.

She shivered under his touch, and the needy ache that had begun long before they even got dressed for the ceremony threatened to undo him before the ritual officially got underway.

He closed his eyes, centering on the people around them. Considering their needs, their dreams. Using the mystical bond he had with the ocean and the people to draw in strength and send it out again. It worked, to a small degree. Only it wasn't the gathered otter folk who filled his awareness most keenly, it was the woman at his side who was easily the most mysterious and the most intimate connection he felt.

Laurin wiggled uncomfortably on the solid wood of the chair. The hard surface had warmed under her bare buttocks, she was happy there was no cushion to sit on—it would have been soaked already by the liquid sneaking from her sex. She squeezed her knees together tighter and sat ramrod straight in an attempt to keep the tiny bits of nothing draped over her breasts strategically lined up.

Whatever fabric they'd skimped on to create her and Matt's costumes had been used for Willam's. Across the staged area, he grinned down at her, as if he knew exactly what she wasn't wearing under her garment.

Which, of course, he did, and that made it all the more sexual when he methodically looked her over. When he turned his head and took in Matt with as thorough an inspection, she hesitated. The first intense scrutiny had made her uncomfortable; the second filled her with an ache deep inside she didn't want to name.

Was she jealous? Perhaps. She reached without thinking to place her hand possessively on her lover's knee.

Willam's grin flashed even larger, and he nodded slowly, as if accepting her motion as a choice.

Oh my God, had she done what Matt had warned her not to do? Had she just agreed to something?

At her side, Matt dropped his fingers over hers. The warmth of his palm on the back of her hand held her in place, trapped against his leg. He leaned over. "They are about to begin. Last chance to chicken out."

She turned her head, their cheeks touching. "As if I could leave now. Everyone would be able to stare at my butt the entire time I walked away."

He kissed her and withdrew, but not before she caught his low laugh.

Laurin blew out a deep breath. It was official—she was in big trouble.

Above her, the night sky had filled with stars, the darkness a charcoal canopy. Off in the distance, the wind shook the treetops gently, rustling them together in time with the constant roar of the surf. There was no confining roof holding her in. If it came down to the worst-case scenario, she could always shift and escape to the sky.

And suddenly, that made everything all right again. Her ability to shift was there to be called on in an instant if needed. Matt was by her side, and she trusted him implicitly and...he was driving her crazy.

Matt had removed his fingers from her hand and now rested them lightly on her thigh, his thumb tracing tiny circles on her flesh.

A wave of heat raced over her that had nothing to do with the temperature, and everything to do with what she unexpectedly wanted. There was going to be a sexy performance tonight? Bring it on. Maybe it was time for her innocent air shifter ways to be woken up.

A horn sounded, long and low, and the intermingling voices dropped to a murmur. Willam stood, his hands raised in the air and the gathered adults all hushed.

After delivering two sharp claps with his hands, Willam sat. There were no words spoken, and Laurin was puzzled. In her tribe, the storyteller would have sung and prayed. The noise generated during ceremonies tied them together and taught the lessons for the next generations to remember.

At her side, Matt stood. He looked over the crowd, and the brush of what she called his shaman senses passed her. Was he testing the response of the people? Preparing them? He nodded once at Willam.

Eager faces turned from staring at the clan leader to waiting for Matt. When he reached down for her hand, she placed her fingers in his hesitantly, shaking slightly. She mentally chastised herself. What outrageous thing did she think he was about to do? She stood at his side willingly, looking out into the crowd as fearlessly as possible, only the flutter of her heartbeat at her throat giving away her nervousness. The gazes of the men in the crowd grew hungry, the women—some appeared jealous, the more mature, eager?

Matt squeezed her fingers briefly before turning her in his arms and cupping her face. He kissed her, an almost chaste brush of his lips. Her magic woke and she trembled at the intense power building inside her. It was as if he'd held a flame to a stick of dynamite, and she wondered exactly how long the wick would turn out to be.

She opened her eyes slowly, catching a flicker of amusement sparkling in his gaze. He motioned for her to sit before joining her, keeping their fingers tangled together.

As one, the rest of the people settled, all attention focused on the center of the stage.

From one side of the dais a form strolled forward—one of the young, unattached women of the community, with a strong body and hair elaborately coiffed about her head. She strutted her way around the edge of the gathering, ignoring the raised platform slightly off-center of the stage. She swung her hips, taking her time to pivot before the young men and undulate her torso sensuously. The diaphanous shift covering her body was somehow far more erotic than if she'd walked on stage totally nude.

In the background, a beat began—not a drum, but something more organic. Pulsing hot and heavy as if the surface of the stage was alive. The woman twirled, her shift rising to expose her limbs before falling again in a curtain. Laurin leaned forward, her own heart synchronizing with the pulse, making her entire body tingle and throb in rhythm.

The sun disappeared completely, the golden orange flames of the torches seeming to leach the color from the sky. Radiant beams danced over the woman, highlighting her dark skin, the swell of her breasts against the fabric. She paused for longer in one place, staring intently into the crowd, her actions slowing and becoming more sexual. Her skin glistened with oil that reflected the flickering torchlight. She tossed her head, raised her hands in the air and turned in a smooth circle. The throbbing in the air increased in tempo, in volume until, with a jerk, she pointed into the crowd and everything froze.

There was complete silence but for the sound of rapid breathing, Laurin's own shaky inhalations loud in her ears.

From where the woman pointed, a young man rose to his feet. Laurin recognized him from her days amidst the clan. Tall, strong-limbed. One of the men who had propositioned her and been totally astounded to be turned down. A path opened before him, allowing him to stride easily to the stage where he took the woman's hand.

And the beat resumed. Louder this time, a staggered cadence that fit the movements of the two on the stage perfectly. They danced, his hands wrapping around her body, intimately caressing her back. Slipping down her waist and hovering over her butt for a split second. The shimmering fabric of her shift moved like moonbeams under his hands' direction. Laurin swallowed hard, feeling a pulse growing within her sex as she watched the performance. His costume was similar to what Matt wore, a scrap of cloth in the front, his buttocks revealed in the back as he turned his partner only feet before them. He too was covered with oil, the edges of his muscles showing cut and strong with the light reflecting off. When he twirled the woman and pressed her back to his front, one hand cupping her breast, a small moan escaped Laurin's lips.

Matt released her fingers and instead caressed the inside of her wrist in a steady motion. She couldn't look away from the stage, but didn't want to miss a single touch Matt offered. Squirming did nothing to ease the ache between her legs, and she snuck her free hand to her lap, casually, as if she simply needed to change position. The gentle weight wasn't enough, and she let her legs open slightly, the cool night air sweeping up her thighs. The cream that had already escaped her core met the air and she shuddered. Wanting more. Needing more.

The dancers twined together, intimate and slow. The woman threw back her head and he held her draped over his arm, her body leaning far enough back her breasts had broken free of the flimsy fabric. When he straightened them to vertical the shift clung to her hips for a second, then pooled on the ground. She stood naked before the crowd, her chest heaving as she gazed into her partner's eyes.

The pulse increased in tempo and volume, and this time Laurin spotted the source. It was the people of the clan. With their feet or hands, they pounded against the stage. Hammering out the rhythm together as if they too were a part of the dance.

Something feral broke free. She'd never seen anything so

profound, so intimate and yet cohesive. Her own feet itched to join in the noise making, but she fought the urge. A tug on her wrist brought her attention to Matt. He stared, the bright blue of his eyes reminding her of the water they'd paddled together the previous week, and it hit her. He was part of it as well, a part of the environment of ecstasy swelling around them, and suddenly it wasn't nearly enough to sit passively and witness the dance.

Matt slid back in his chair and pulled her easily toward him, settling her on his lap. His erection bulged against her hip, his hands tender on her body as he adjusted position. Laurin leaned into his warmth, the bare skin of her back meeting his naked chest, and she sighed with contentment.

His touch melted her defenses, and when the side of his hand brushed the bottom of her breast, she didn't protest at all. Matt's lips touched her ear, his whisper barely breaking the vocal silence. "Join me in the celebration."

She looked over the crowd. All eyes were fixed on the duo in the center of the stage where the woman had one of her long limbs wrapped around the man's hip as he held her against his groin. A shiver went through Laurin—electric heat hit her core and her emptiness became too apparent.

She and Matt sat in full sight of the clan, yet for all the attention they received, they could have been completely private. Unable to deny what her body begged for, Laurin turned her head to capture his lips for an instant. "I will celebrate with you."

His body heated under her, as if her words were the catalyst for the next step they would take together. He slid one hand up her body, one down, and sudden pleasure poured through her limbs. A single digit stroked her slit. His thumb and forefinger teased one nipple. Laurin closed her eyes to concentrate, only to have Matt nuzzle her neck until she focused on him.

"Watch. There's more. See it, feel it. Celebrate with my people."

His eyes held a hint of laughter, and more. Something she couldn't stare at for very long—it was too powerful and breathtakingly beautiful.

She nodded, and then kissed him. Full on, lust filled. A tangle of tongues and teeth that combined with his touch took her to the edge of a climax in a single bound.

He broke away from her and she turned back to the stage, ready to witness the conclusion of the dance. Hoping it would be over soon so she could take Matt back to their cabin and fall into bed with him for the rest of the night.

Where she expected to see two people, there were now three.

Chapter Six

Laurin's gaze stuttered over the naked bodies, slowly untangling the connections between the limbs and the torsos. The man who had danced earlier sat on the large covered platform that now filled center stage, his hand grasping the woman's hips as he mouthed her breasts. At her back, another male had joined in, pressing kisses along the line of her shoulder. He reached around to splay one hand over her belly, the other cupping one full mound, lifting it as if an offering to the one seated before her.

Matt copied the motion, teasing her with his fingertips, massaging her breast with his hand over the tiny scrap of fabric clinging to her skin. It was torture to have him so close, and yet so far. She took one more rapid glance at the crowds. There was no doubt—all attention was on center stage, and rightly so. Laurin watched in fascination and with growing lust as the seated man lay back and the dancer crawled over him, her hips centered over his face.

Oh my God, he licked her. Touched the woman intimately, just as Matt's finger stroked Laurin's sex. The trembling in Laurin's limbs increased, and when she realized exactly who the new male arrival on the stage was, she shook hard enough Matt grabbed onto both her thighs, locking her against him.

James danced around the two bodies touching on the

platform. His erection thrust out from his body, but he danced as if unaware his arousal was evident to all. When he turned and faced her and Matt, his face clearly showed his desire.

Laurin squirmed, attempting to close her legs. Matt restrained her, his touch against her core continuing, his lips and teeth lapping and nibbling on the curve of her ear. He slipped a finger into the wetness of her sex at the same instant he slipped his tongue into her ear and she cried out as her body responded. A burst of pleasure, connecting from top to bottom, exploded—unexpected yet completely welcome. Her sexual tension didn't fade, but slipped from being painfully aroused to anxiously waiting for the next, higher level of gratification to arrive.

Matt spread his knees. Since her limbs were draped over his, the motion opened her wide, her bare crotch facing the stage. Laurin hesitated before reaching to tug the rest of her skirt out of the way. A sense of being incredibly wicked hit as James stared directly at her from only a few paces away.

Matt whispered in her ear, the warmth of his breath fluttering past her cheek. "You are beautiful, Laurin. All of you, not only your body. But tonight, let your body be what you share for others' pleasure."

She tensed. Was he going to let James touch her? She couldn't—

His lips touched her temple, his words coming quickly to stay her fears. "Peace. You are mine. I am yours. Only watch, and allow the others to witness your passion as well."

Matt kissed her lips, so gentle and intimate, even as his fingers stroked her clit, dipping into her core and pulling up her cream to ease the motion of his fingers over the sensitive bud. Sexual tension rallied, small strokes of electricity flying from wherever he touched to congregate deep inside and add to the building pressure.

The thumping against the stage stilled again and she snapped her head back to see what it meant. Even as Matt had played her body, the dancers had turned to more erotic connections. The woman perched over one man, her slowly descending hips angled exactly right for Laurin to see his erection piercing her sex. Small pumps with her hips echoed by the crowd's hands on the ground, the beat resuming as the pulse of their joining was copied among the clan. Matt's fingers brushing her clit weren't enough, and Laurin dropped her own hand to rub more firmly, needing a little more to fly.

Watching another couple have sex was incredibly arousing.

Matt leaned forward, tilting her until her hips rose into the air, and then—

"Oh...Matt." She whispered the words, uncertain if she should speak or not. Unsure what the rules were. She stared back over her shoulder to catch his eye as the tip of his cock pressed to her labia, and he rocked, coating himself in her cream.

"Yes?" he asked.

Laurin waited until the next pass when he was lined up perfectly, then gripped his forearms and pulled, plunging his entire length into her body. She was far too ready to need any more foreplay.

Full of hard, stretching power, she rested, letting him take back control. Laurin squeezed her inner muscles and tore a gasp from his lips.

She turned back to the stage, ready for anything. Anything except to see James present the tip of his rigid cock to the woman's ass and press into that tight passage. Torchlight flickered off glistening skin—the oil from earlier now coating their entire bodies. Matt seemed to swell inside her as she clenched in response to what she witnessed.

Two men taking the woman at the same time—the act was never spoken of among the air people. Since coming to the coast, she'd heard of it, but thought it would be awkward, and ugly. Painful at the least and a turn-off at the worst. Instead, the sight fed the fire inside hard enough to send her desire flaring upward. The woman sang out in pleasure between her lovers, her face bright with delight. The pounding racket from the clan increased, the thrusts of the men alternating into her body.

Matt fisted Laurin's hips and brought her down on his cock hard enough to force a gasp from her. Again and again he took her in time with the lovers on stage, in time with the pounding heartbeat of the community. When another male joined the central gathering, Laurin thought her body would burst. There was too much energy in the area, Matt's power spilling out, her own magic escaping in small eddies that swirled around them.

She could take no more—her every resistance had been torn down. Her natural reticence to witness such a public display was erased by the beauty of the connection. Laurin closed her eyes and concentrated on Matt, bringing a small measure of privacy to their lovemaking.

Silence fell again and her eyes flew open, needing to see what it foretold this time. Matt pulled her back, his hands cupping her breasts, then moving to play at the apex of her clit. Spinning her lust into a frenzy as the third man circled the joined trio, reaching out his hand to skim his fingers lightly over their bodies. He stepped beside the platform and stoked his cock, fisting from tip to base.

Thump.

Another stroke of his hand, and another beat rang against the ground as the crowd picked up the rhythm. Each thrust he made bought the tempo to a higher speed, the men entering the woman's body joining in, and when the standing male approached the woman, she threw back her head and laughed out loud. Opened her jaw wide, and took his cock into her mouth.

The dancer was filled to completion, three men worshipping her body, three sets of hands stroking and priming her. The passion in the center of the stage glowed like a miniature sun. Laurin was no longer shocked, or embarrassed, or any of the things she'd imagined she should feel. Fire licked her skin, filled her core, sparkled along her fingertips and exploded out from her.

She'd had enough watching, and all she needed was to reach a final conclusion.

With Matt.

She rose from his lap, painfully empty as his cock pulled from the shelter of her sex. Laurin turned to face him, reached up to strip off the bikini top. She cupped her own breasts and his gaze fixed on her hands. He ignored the ceremony, ignored the noises rising on the air as the tempo of feet on the ground was joined by what could be nothing less than the echo from bodies connecting. The slap of skin meeting skin rang loudly, and yet his attention remained solely on her.

Laurin peeled away the tiny skirt to stand naked before him. Seeing his attentive fascination made her forget, and yet not forget. She knew where she stood. She knew there was the possibility that others were even now staring at her naked butt.

She didn't give a damn. He was hers to claim. Laurin straddled him, surrounded his shaft with her hand and stroked until a moan of pleasure fled his lips. She held his cock vertical and eased him into her body.

So good, so exactly what she needed. Matt adjusted her

and leaned in to catch a nipple between his teeth. She gave a little scream. Pain and pleasure wrapped around each other, and she arched into him, wanting more. His fingers dug into her hips as he moved her, helping her to rise and fall, spearing them together. One hand slid to cover her butt, his lean fingers tracing the line between her ass cheeks. When he rubbed the tight star hidden there, she gasped. When he pressed in to the knuckle, sparks exploded behind her eyes, and she was lost.

All around them magic and nature blended together in a perfect finish. Her orgasm seemed to make the stars pop out brighter in the sky, a flash of northern lights shimmering in the air. The whoosh of an ocean breeze fluttered through the gathering, ruffling her hair and cooling the heated surface of her skin. All the time he pumped into her, the thickness of his cock forcing her to accept additional shards of pleasure after she'd already experienced more than she'd imagined possible.

"Laurin... Oh, yes." Matt flexed his hips one last time before stilling, a drop of sweat trickling down his temple as his cock jerked within her. A backlash of aftershocks took her and she quivered in his arms. There was nothing in the universe but him and her, and all the stars swirling against their skin, depositing desire and lust with each flicker. He wrapped her close, their skin sticking together as they clung together tightly, her climax going on and on.

She collapsed against his chest and let him support her, the loud thumping in her ears seeming out of place until she realized it was the sound of Matt and her heartbeats alone. The clan's rhythmic contribution had ended, although she wasn't sure exactly when. They remained seated, Matt's hand roaming over her shoulders, her back. Resting lightly on her hips.

That had been the most incredible experience of her life. A yawn escaped and he laughed quietly.

"Did I wear you out?"

Silence surrounded them. A flash of recollection hit and her face heated. She'd ridden Matt like a bull in front of the entire clan. "Is everyone still here?" she whispered.

He smoothed the back of his knuckles against her cheek. "Would it matter?"

Yes. *No.* She lowered her head and stared at him from under her lashes and he grinned.

"You can peek. It's safe."

She turned slowly, her ears alert for the sounds of the clan. There was nothing except the continued sound of lovemaking from the center of the stage. The four participants lay curled together on the massive platform, hands still stroking. Mouths connecting.

The entire area around the stage was empty, only six torches remaining to light the area.

"Where did everyone go? Why didn't I hear them?" Laurin whispered the words, not wanting to interrupt the foursome.

"They left after the ceremony was complete. I imagine they left rapidly with things on their minds."

She peeked at him. A wide grin split his handsome face. "You don't know for sure when they left?"

He shook his head. "I was distracted."

Warm contentment filled her. She hadn't been the only one then.

There was no chance to escape the kiss he dragged her into. Not that she wanted to, but they couldn't sit there all night, naked and kissing.

Could they?

A purr of contentment followed by a sharp needy gasp made her twirl her head to seek the source. James had his face

133

buried between the woman's legs as her other lovers stroked and suckled her breasts. Impossibly, another streak of desire hit. How could she possibly feel the urge for any more sex after that incredible climax she'd just experienced?

"Are they going to have sex all night long?" Aching need lingered in her mind and yet now that she wasn't in the flush of desire, embarrassment as well.

Matt used his hand to turn her face to his. "They will. Tradition states the longer they last, the more fruitful the coming year will be."

Such dedication to hedonistic pleasure. She squeezed her legs together at the thought of three men taking her over and over.

He placed his arms under her limbs and stood, carrying her easily. Laurin rested her head on his chest and wished she were brave enough to ask if they could stay and watch for longer. Her discomfort with feeling such a desire warred with the level of curiosity screaming inside her core. She was truly becoming the most forward creature, but that seemed to be what Matt needed, and her part of their relationship bargain was to be there for him, as he'd been for her.

She held back a gasp of shock when Matt stopped beside the platform and lowered her to stand with him. They stood, naked, as the dancers—the lovers—rolled apart and rose to their feet. Laurin stared as all four, one after another, kissed Matt full on the lips. He smiled at them all, nodding his acceptance.

In unison they turned to her.

She waited, uncertain what to do. The female dancer stepped forward, pressing their unclothed bodies together in a hug that felt far softer and warmer than any feminine connection Laurin had ever experienced before. A light kiss landed on her lips before the woman withdrew. The first male dancer bowed more formally, scooping up her fingers and kissing them. The other man did the same, then backed away, regaining the platform with the woman and falling back into each other's grasps.

Only James remained. Laurin snuck a peek at Matt, her hand sneaking involuntarily to cover her chest. James's grin widened.

At her side, Matt spoke quietly. "Laurin, this ass wants to give you honor as well. Will you let him?"

She stepped closer, seeking the protection of his warm body. "What exactly is he intending on doing?"

Matt's hand brushed her back, coming to rest intimately on her hip. "Nothing but a kiss. Unless you want more."

Her head whipped around and she stared at him. "But surely you don't want me to... I mean—"

Matt's grip tightened. "No, I don't want him to do anything more than complete the ceremonial ritual, but it's your right to accept more."

"No. Nothing more." The words exploded out, and she watched James's expression fade from one of anticipation to resignation.

"Ah, well, a fellow's got to hope, you know."

Matt growled lightly. "Go on, and don't take all day."

James dipped his head politely, then reached out a hand to Laurin. She glanced hesitantly at Matt. He nodded, and she took a steadying breath and placed her fingers in James's. He kissed them briefly before tugging her closer and nestling her tight against him. Her naked skin had cooled in the brief time they'd stood talking, and a physical connection between them flickered like embers under a fine layer of ashes. Banked heat, waiting to flare up with the slightest provocation. He slipped his fingers around her neck and pressed their lips together.

Deep disappointment and blessed relief hit simultaneously. The man was sexy, and giving, and...just didn't turn her on. The thought of having another man touch her while she made love with Matt—that didn't seem as far-fetched as she'd believed at the start of the evening. There was something simmering far below the surface that had been extremely turned on watching the performance.

But not with James.

The otter shifter released her with a sigh, shaking his head sorrowfully. He clicked his tongue and turned to Matt. "Ah, mate, you've found yourself a fine one with this lady."

Matt surrounded her, taking possession and hiding her frame against his. "I have, and you remember it."

James tilted his head cockily. "Well, if you'll not take me as a third right now, then I'd best return to my party."

He spun and strode the few paces back to where the others of his clan had resumed their lovemaking. Laurin had had enough. She tucked her face into Matt's neck and shook as the whole evening crashed in on her.

His lips touched her temple. Tender. Warm. "Let me get you home."

She let him take her by the hand and lead her back to their cabin, and all the time that word spun in her brain. *Home.*

It was becoming clearer that meant less a physical location and more wherever Matt happened to be.

Chapter Seven

The tide would turn in a few short hours. Matt moved smoothly over the deck as he made the final adjustments he needed to ready the *Stormchild* to sail. There were extra bodies scattered all over the ship—members of the clan lending a hand bringing his and Laurin's possessions on board, as well as stealing a final opportunity to snoop on the shaman and his lady's private space.

Matt had never looked forward to moving to a new community more in his life.

"Ho, the ship." Willam stood at the railing, peering toward the wheelhouse. "Is your woman already on board?"

Probably hoped Matt would somehow forget and leave without her. As if that was possible. Since the night of the ceremony they'd been linked even closer. Not only in their physical reactions, but it was as if the ceremony had triggered some kind of revelation in both of them.

"She's with the children, saying farewell and giving last-minute assignments."

Willam nodded. He clapped his hands and a group of men appeared, carrying a heavy chest and lowering it carefully to the decking.

Matt strode over. "What is this?"

The otter chief grinned. "Your wedding gift from my people."

"But we can't—"

The man's hand rose regally to stop Matt's protests. "You honored us by being the first community you visited after becoming one. We honor you as is your right and our privilege."

Willam crossed his arms over his bulky chest. Stubborn, good-hearted fool. There was nothing Matt needed from this clan, but to turn the gift away?

He bowed. "We give you thanks."

Willam smiled, his teeth flashing white. "You're welcome."

The clan leader turned to the dock and clapped again, and another group scurried on board. Matt eyed the second chest with trepidation. Generosity was one thing, but he had to be able to stow all these new items safely and the *Stormchild* wasn't built like a barge. "Are there many more, sir?"

A loud laugh escaped the man. "This is for Laurin. She can thank me properly the next time you return."

There was far too much innuendo implied in that comment, but Matt chose to let it go. The leader turned and walked away without another glance, leaving Matt silently amused as he directed the clan men where to store the chests.

The rest of their leave-taking was far less dramatic than their arrival. Laurin arrived within five minutes of her expected time, the gathering of little ones who had escorted her scattering back to their mothers as she made her way over the plank to reach the deck. He waved, and finished his prep, watching her every chance he got until she ducked below and disappeared from his sight. When she returned topside she wore a thin tank top, her arms bare to the sunshine and the rising breeze. She leaned back on the cabin house, her dark eyes fixed on him as he took them out of the marina. A dozen of the clan still sprawled naked on the deck and she raised a brow

138

and indicated them with her head.

"It's okay," he called out. "They're simply looking for an adventure."

She crossed her arms. "How long is this adventure supposed to last?"

"Not long." The *Stormchild* broke free from the harbor, the waves rising to greet the keel and the clan shouted in delight. One after another they raced to the prow and leapt from the deck, shifting in midair to land with a splash in their otter forms.

Laurin rushed forward, laughter escaping as she wrapped an arm around Matt's waist. "They are the most rambunctious, the most fun loving, and the most alive of any of the People of the Sea."

Matt nuzzled under her ear with his nose, keeping one arm wrapped around her waist and the other firmly on the tiller. "And they can totally drive a person insane."

She smiled at him, her eyes widening as she stared over his shoulder. "Shit. I think we picked up a stowaway."

Matt twisted his head and swore. The last thing he'd expected, the last person he wanted to see. "James. You sea dog. What the hell are you doing?"

His friend pushed off the tarp that had covered him and stood, running a hand through his dark hair. He was naked, as usual, and grinned at Laurin while wiggling his brows. "Just thought I'd check one more time if you needed me for anything."

"Go."

Matt roared it out at the same instant Laurin seconded his command, pointing back toward the village, her other fist firmly planted on her hip.

James raised his hands in entreaty. "Fine, I'll leave. But

you'll need a third sometime. I wanted you to know I'm available..."

Matt didn't think of using his shaman power. In fact, he was sure he had a tight grip on his reflexes, but suddenly James slid across the deck, hit the railing and tipped over backward. The size of the resulting splash indicated the man hadn't had time to shift to otter before reaching the water's surface.

Hell. He didn't know Laurin had the ability to do that. Matt twisted to stare at her in surprise. "Remind me not to piss you off."

"Me? What did I do? I didn't think that was a very nice way for you to treat your friend, even if he's got sex on the brain."

"That wasn't me." He let go of the tiller and went to peer over the railing. Otters danced and played around the *Stormchild*, leaping the wake in some crazy imitation of their dolphin cousins.

Laurin's face was white. "Then how...?"

He motioned her to wheelhouse, switching the controls and preparing to sail. "We can talk about it more when we get underway. But I think, perhaps, your powers and mine decided James had had enough of our time."

"We did that together?"

"It's the only explanation." She looked so concerned he paused to smooth a hand down her arm, comforting her. "It's okay. As strange as it seems, there was no harm done by it. And don't worry about James—trust me, it's not the first time he's ever been kicked out from where he wasn't requested."

She gave a laugh and nodded, kissing his cheek before moving to get out of his way.

Laurin tucked the last of her things into the compartments in the forward berth. Leaving any community was usually bittersweet, but this was the first time she'd actually not looked forward to her next destination.

The journey there with Matt—time with some privacy—was all that was on her mind.

She'd never realized how very lonely she'd become over the past years. Moving from community to community had ensured her secrecy, but had also never allowed her to find anyone to confide in. This past month having Matt by her side had been a delight. Someone to talk to in the evenings, someone to bounce ideas off, even if it was in the stolen moments between his busy schedule and her own.

The cold empty ache in her core was warmer these days, and she would willingly confess it was because of Matt's presence in her life.

She made her way toward the deck, stopping in the galley to put on a kettle of water for coffee. The tidy kitchen area made her smile—everything about the *Stormchild* reminded her of Matt. Organized, neat, and yet full of energy and surprises. His very presence was felt in the surroundings. She stirred sweetener into their drinks and covered the mugs with travel lids to take topside with her.

He was unfurling the spinnaker, aligning it with wind and letting the *Stormchild* move slowly with the rising breeze.

"Need me to do anything?" she called out.

He tossed a brilliant smile at her over his shoulder even as he shook his head. "Nearly done."

Laurin put his coffee into a cup holder alongside the aft seating before wandering forward to face the direction of their travel. Sunlight danced on the ocean's surface, tiny sparkles flashing as waves curled and broke before their prow.

Traveling forward. Headed for new destinations. She had children to teach all along the coast, with adjustments to make to fit her schedules with Matt's. Every place they stopped she'd find new delights to entertain her. The ship dipped and rose, cradled by the ocean. It reminded her of flying—of the rise and fall when she soared on the wind currents, and suddenly the similarities between their worlds seemed far greater than the differences.

A pair of arms wrapped around her, Matt's cheek pressed close to hers. His breath warmed her as he spoke. "You happy?"

She nodded. "I had a wonderful time with the otter folk. The teaching went well and..." How much could she say? How much did she want to admit? The connection between them grew deeper all the time, but she still didn't understand why.

He twisted her to face him and slanted his mouth over hers. Kissing away her fears that lingered on the surface. When she would have moved against him, though, he withdrew, brushing his fingertips over her lips. "And what? You can't start a sentence like that and not finish it."

Laurin stared at the horizon, the bright water meeting the endless sky. "We still don't know why we're together."

"Do we need to know?"

She frowned. "Of course."

"Right now? Isn't it enough to know that we're headed in the proper direction?" He cupped her face in his hand, the ocean she always saw reflected in his eyes flooding her soul as he stared back. "We don't know what tomorrow will bring, but for now, I am content that we are together. Not just physically, but in all the ways that count." He adjusted their position, turning his back to the wind. "I admire you, Laurin. The advances you accomplished with the children in a limited time—extraordinary. The way you handled the clan and their idiosyncrasies in a polite and yet direct manner—political genius."

She laughed. "Yes, finding new ways to ask for my clothes to be returned always involves diplomatic sweet talk."

They exchanged smiles, the warmth of their bodies melding together like a soft and comfortable blanket. Then the bright light in his eyes deepened to hunger. She saw his passion rise and knew it was for her. Because of her. His voice, when he spoke again, had dropped a level, turning thick with desire.

"You put aside your natural modesty and honored me with your body. That meant your mind and soul willingly gave as well, and I will never forget it."

A shiver ran along her skin as his magic washed her. A blessing. A promise. Her own powers stirred and meshed with his—creating an almost intoxicating blend.

He kissed her again, this time an increased urgency accompanying his touch. She fell under his spell, letting her own needs surface. They could have carried on, been carried away into the most natural consequences if the wind hadn't chosen that moment to gust, flapping the sails wildly.

Matt stepped back, his gaze stroking her skin even as he moved to the ropes to fasten them tighter. "I'm not done with you."

"Promises, promises."

She danced away as he made a teasing grab in her direction. Laurin slipped out of reach, sliding closer to the wheelhouse, only to discover a large chest she hadn't seen before tucked against the wall. The clasps opened easily and she nudged the lid upward, a flash of brightness hitting her eye.

On top of a layer of fabric rested a picture frame. Tiny pieces of abalone and minute shell fragments intertwined in the most intricate design, forming a triad of chains woven in relief

143

against the vertical and cross posts. In the center there was a picture of her and Matt, the sun backlighting them. She stood on the rocky outcrop outside the village, her hand extended toward him. He was reaching up toward her, his head tilted back, feet firmly placed on the beach. Their fingers had just touched, the sun shining like a spotlight on the connection point.

Her heart skipped a beat.

She stared for the longest time, only subtly aware of the ship's movements as Matt guided them. When they'd set out together, not so very long ago, it had been a relationship built completely on mutual attraction. The mystical attachment that followed had been unexpected, but he was right—all they had to do right now was acknowledge it existed. The *why* would eventually make itself clear.

But there was another emotion growing. She clutched the picture to her chest and twisted to stare at Matt as he turned them into the shelter of a bay for the night. He guided the *Stormchild* confidently, as he'd dealt with so many other issues over the past days. He'd said he admired her...

There was plenty to admire about him as well.

The splash of the anchor hitting the water woke her from her reverie and she started. He approached smoothly, his expression indulgent and pleased.

"You found our gifts from the otter clan. Is there something that pleases you?"

She nodded, then held out the picture. Laurin waited to see his response, anxiety fluttering inside—maybe he wouldn't see the significance of the shot. He knelt beside her and brushed her hair behind one ear. He cupped her neck, touching their foreheads together. They stayed that way for a long time, their breaths synchronizing, bodies swaying slightly with the gentle movement of the ship as she rested for the night.

He tilted her chin and Laurin saw it in his eyes. He understood. A rush of emotion hit her and she wondered how fear and joy, uncertainty and confidence, could all be present simultaneously, but somehow, they were.

Matt brushed his lips against hers, speaking with the whisper of the wind. "We will move forward together. Wherever this path takes us."

Laurin smiled and leaned into his frame, tucking into the protection of his body. Accepting the worship of his hands, the steadfastness of his caring.

The water's path was uncertain, but she'd take the journey. With him.

Silent Storm

Dedication

Darling Kate. You make me happy, even though the miles seem to pop up between us as if cast by some twisted magical curse. Nano-cruise has an eternal place in my heart, along with your smile and your sheer enthusiasm for the horseshoes I've found.

You're a special, special lady. Write your heart out.

Chapter One

All around her, towering mountains descended sharply into the sparkling waters of the Pacific. Their ragged surfaces were torn as if a giant hand had grabbed desperate snatches from the earth, leaving behind nothing but thin air and harsh ridges of granite exposed to the brilliant August sun. Along the waterline, where the tide's highest marks had ripped and torn the land, sun-bleached logs lay in tangled heaps, the exposed roots of massive cedars now tormented remains of once majestic trees.

The world kept changing. It was inevitable.

Laurin Marshall guided her kayak along the inlet, letting the crisp morning air fill her lungs, seeking a moment's respite from her internal turmoil. Her mind was filled with images, emotions, and uncertain longings. Two years had passed since she'd deserted her mountain clan to find a place among the water shifters known as the People of the Sea. Only a couple months ago her life had been radically transformed again.

She dipped one side of the double paddle, then the other, moving her arms in a smooth, even rhythm. Trying to let the pace of her heart and the motion of the routine soothe her aching soul.

There were so many things she loved about this life. The water, the proximity to the coastal mountain ranges. The way the water reflected the emotion of the seasons in the colors filling the seemingly endless sky.

She couldn't get enough of the beauty before her. So different, and in some ways raw and stark, compared to the Rockies where she'd grown up. Oh, the mountains of her home reached even higher to the sky, and when she flew, shifted into one of the forms of the People of the Air, it seemed there was nothing between her and the stars. But here, the ocean spoke to her. It had a voice and a song—poles apart from the wind in the pine trees or the flutter of a breeze against a mountain lake.

The sea was vibrant and alive, and she'd fallen totally in love with it.

Laurin paused in her paddling, letting the kayak drift as she rested out of the wind in a small bay. Around her a pod of dolphins surfaced, a couple of the younger ones sliding cheekily alongside her craft, their pectoral fins slapping the water beside the gunwales and splashing her. She laughed aloud and held up a hand to ward off the worst of the attack.

The matriarch of the group surfaced and sang out, and Laurin wished again she could understand what she was saying. The female, with her beautiful smile, dipped her head then submerged, the rest of the pod following. An immature male rose one final time into the air, twisting and landing beside the kayak. Laurin was instantly drenched.

She had to smile. The sea and her people were amazing, even though she'd never been so waterlogged in her life. Part of the downside of being partner to the shaman of the Pacific Inside Passage. Laurin picked up her paddle and headed for the thin strip of sand visible just ahead of her. There were dry clothes in the aft compartment, and if she'd read Matt's note correctly, there should be a relaxing break waiting ahead.

He joined her on the beach. Six feet of brown skin, firm

muscles and a grin that was all for her. The neat khaki shorts he wore did nothing but draw her attention to his bare chest and the ridge of his abdominal muscles carving down under the beltline.

"Did you have a good paddle?" Matt pulled the prow of the kayak far up on the sand so she could step out onto solid ground. His thoughtfulness warmed her, even though she scarcely needed to worry about staying dry. He guided her with a steady hand as he helped her from the cockpit. "Laurin, why are you soaked?"

Because your people gave me homage? "Enthusiastic teenager, I think."

Matt Jentry wrapped his arms around her and held her tight, his even heartbeat under her ear now so familiar and so right, she could barely imagine not having him close by. Somewhere near, to touch, to talk to. She glanced up at his beautiful face, firm cheekbones, strong jawline. She couldn't imagine never getting to taste him again.

"Well, that's an intriguing look. You going to share what's on your mind to go with that enticing expression?" His voice was husky and low, and her need for him blossomed into full desire.

She couldn't imagine life without his lovemaking either. She reached up and brought their mouths together.

He kissed her softly, placing a series of light bites along her lower lip, dragging the surface into his mouth and letting it go. She explored with her tongue, teasing his lips, his teeth, his tongue. All the while his hands were busy at her buttons, her waistband. Stripping off her clothes, baring her to the elements. She willingly did the same for him, thrilling at the encounter of her fingers against his torso. The slight breeze brushed her skin, and she wondered again at the remote locations he always managed to find. There were no clans close to this inlet, no human eyes to see them naked and entwined.

Matt lifted her in his arms without taking his lips from hers. She closed her eyes and simply soaked in the experience. The warmth of his touch versus the cool of the blanket he lowered her to. The heat of his kisses, now descending to worship her breasts and tease her nipples to tight peaks. The breeze stroked a cold finger over the wet tip and it tightened even more.

He hummed in admiration. "I did have a picnic lunch arranged, but I'm not sure if I have the strength to wait. Are you hungry?"

Laurin stared up at her lover of two months, the man with whom she had a mystical connection they were still trying to figure out. A mental and emotional connection beyond the ordinary—that only grew stronger the longer they were together. "I'm always hungry for you."

They moved together with an easy rhythm, the first fumbling moments of becoming lovers seemingly far in the past. It was straightforward, but not boring, the passion between them rising fast and staying strong. Whether it was because their magic clicked, or because somehow they truly fit together well, Laurin didn't know. And at this time, didn't care to analyze.

She needed him. As always.

Matt pulled her close, stroking his hands down her naked torso. He cupped her butt and slid her over him so they were centered on the blanket. It took him a second to sit upright before pressing her backward slightly to expose her breasts to his attention. His lips fastened around one tip, drawing a string of desire through her entire being, an echoing pulse beginning in her core. Each suckle triggered a responding internal throb, and she moaned, dragging her fingers through his dark hair to hold him close.

Receiving his full attention was a humbling experience. Laurin had never felt this way about previous lovers, had never had a connection that went deeper than the physical pleasure they shared. With Matt, his steamy touch was wrapped up in the layers of emotion she felt from him. It mixed with traces of thoughts that tangled her mind, and there were moments she didn't know if it was her ideas or his driving her crazy with desire.

Warm skin, wet lips, the hard surface of his shaft between them. Laurin adjusted her legs to kneel on either side of his thighs, her sex covering his rigid erection. She rose and lowered slowly, letting him slip along her core as the moisture from her body coated his cock.

Images of him slipping into her—of the pleasure he felt—rolled back through the strange and powerful link they shared. Combined with the scent of the sea, between the remembrances of the past times they'd made love and this current time, the sensory overload grew almost devastating. It wasn't simply the touch of his hands massaging her breasts, there was the lingering sensation of his mouth, and an echo of a time in the past when he'd pinched and teased her nipples until she could barely think.

It was lovemaking with layers of memories, and each time it grew more powerful. When Matt grasped her hips and adjusted her so his erection slid into her depths, she wasn't sure how much of the pleasure was from this occasion and how much from the past.

"Matt...oh. Oh, yes."

He wrapped one arm around her back and brought their torsos together, pulsing his hips lightly, more a rocking together than a powerful thrusting into her body.

It was still impossible to stop the reaction of her body to him. They fit—and yet...

An undeniable sensation of sadness burst through her. Laurin slammed it behind a mental wall and tried to deny it existed. She stared into his bright blue orbs. He returned her gaze without blinking, the emotion on his face making it impossible to look away.

"Do you see it?" he whispered. He moved their bodies together, with another rock, another slide. "Do you feel it?"

Racing headlong into her climax, tumbling into passion, Laurin trembled. It was more than the delights of joining together, under the heat of the sun and with the wind kissing their skin. Matt opened to her, flooding her mind with images from his viewpoint—the instant spark of interest he always experienced as she flirted with him. The expression on her face as she lay sated beside him.

He poured his reactions into her and Laurin's breath caught in her throat. Powerful, yes, even overwhelming to comprehend how much he cared for her. How much he thought of her and wanted the best for her.

She wrapped her arms around his back and twisted, pulling him on top. The blanket was cool beneath her back, protecting them from the ravages of the sandy beach. His cock nestled deeper into her body, filling her, teasing all the sensitive places inside. Equally filled, her heart pounded with the realization he kept nothing secret—shared all he thought of her, all she meant to him.

He loved her.

Matt drew his hips back, then pressed into her again. Her body welcomed his advance, slick with need. His lips found hers, and as they kissed, that small part she kept separated from him trembled to be released.

Another kiss landed, this time on her cheek. His voice was raw and deep with his passion. "Do you hear it, Laurin? Do you hear what my body is telling you? What my mind and soul want you to know?"

Oh God. He plunged in again and again, the pace slow and even, her heart pounding faster than his intimate thrusts. She still couldn't answer, couldn't...

"Do you understand? I offer you everything, willingly. I'm yours, Laurin."

Mine—she mouthed the word against his skin. It was easy to see the ways he gave her love, with all the caring and sharing. Every touch of his hand and the quiet of their evenings together—so different but so clear in making her feel the truth of his emotion.

Why was it so hard to let go of her final fear?

Above her, he stilled. They remained connected, his shaft buried deep in her body. Their minds touched, memories swirled, and yet...

"Laurin?"

Tears lashed her eyes and she pushed aside her apprehension. It wasn't the time to deal with it. It wasn't the place, and he deserved none of her bitter struggle to mar this moment. She opened the part of her mind she'd been hiding from him, only keeping that one secret place buried deep.

"I see, I feel. I know. Oh, Matt...you are too good to me."

"Not possible, it's only what you deserve."

Moving slowly, now faster. Rocking together, hips connecting and withdrawing. Skin on skin, minds brushing, breasts aching. Heart breaking. Laurin accepted his gift and returned it with everything she could. She shared her fascination with his magic, the way his role as a shaman was not a part of him, but him. The gratitude she felt for his place in her life, his protection, his openness, and most of all his love.

She did love him. Almost frighteningly so. She clutched his shoulders and arched under him, taking him into her body, accepting him into her mind. Flashing into the pleasure of release at the same moment he did, their bodies in tune and one.

They both cried out, Laurin reveling in the delight he always brought her, the physical rightness of being with him. Even as he pulsed within her, his seed filling her, the connection between their bodies remaining, Matt brought their lips together for another earth-shattering kiss. When they finally lay, breathing hard on the blanket, Laurin's vision was blurred.

"Wow." The sky spun overhead, continuing aftershocks of pleasure rioting through her system.

He laughed softly, rising up on one elbow to smile down at her. Laurin sighed in contentment, lifting her fingers to trace his jawline. Matt's eyes crinkled at the corners. "You okay? You seemed to disappear for a minute or two—that's not good for a guy's ego."

Laurin soothed him, kissing his lips tenderly. Opened herself to allow how much she cared for him to wash over them both. "I'm sorry. You know I'm guilty of thinking too hard at times."

Matt nodded. "If you can analyze a situation from a new direction, you will. Or make some charts."

"Charts are awesome."

They grinned at each other. Laurin let a slow sigh of relief escape as Matt rolled away and helped her to her feet without pushing for any further explanation. She needed to deal with her concerns, but postcoital? Her emotions were still too raw. Besides, it really was her issue, not anything that was his fault.

They gathered their scattered clothing with an easy companionship. Matt shook the sand from each item before dressing. Laurin chose to retreat to the kayak to find her dry clothing. Matt pulled out a picnic basket, then proceeded to impress her stomach with his cooking as much as he'd dazzled her body with his lovemaking.

In spite of her attentive companion, and the gorgeous setting, her mind kept wandering back to her dilemma, and as they packed up the remains of the picnic lunch, she realized she couldn't carry on this way. It wasn't fair to either of them.

"Matt, can I ask you something?"

"Of course."

"What do you think of me taking a bit of a holiday?"

He took his time to seal the container in his hands before tucking it into a kayak bag. "That depends," he said slowly. "Are you talking about a holiday from teaching or a holiday from...me?"

Oh damn. One of the troubles with being so intimately connected with a shaman—it was difficult to keep secrets. "My tour of summer schools will be over in a couple weeks. The students who are studying via satellite are on a year-round schedule—they'll have a semester break then as well, so I'll have no teaching commitments."

He nodded, his observant gaze flashing over her. "And me?"

Laurin took a deep breath. She reached out and laid a gentle hand on his arm. "Matt, I think I love you."

There was a spark in his eyes, but his smile seemed forced. "How come that came out sounding as if it makes you sad?"

She moistened her lips, searching for the right words. Ones

157

that would make this better. Unfortunately, she had no idea what words those would be.

"Laurin." He held out his hand and she went into his arms eagerly, willing to hide her face against his chest, seeking comfort, wishing she'd never given him any pain. She did love him. She did, that had become crystal clear over the past month.

But was it enough?

"I see you. I don't think you even know you're doing it." Matt lifted her chin until their eyes met. "The way you stare into the sky with such longing. I don't understand why you avoid flying."

Her heart ached. "I'm afraid."

He frowned. "Afraid of the sky? Of shifting? Laurin, there will be no further challenges from anyone who sought you before. You are free from the fears that sent you into hiding two years ago. I swear."

"It's not that. I'm afraid that if I fly too often I'll—" Her words choked to a stop. Could she ever commit to being with him forever? Forsake the mountains of her childhood and all of her family?

Her people?

It had never been an issue until now, not until Matt. She cradled his face tenderly in her palms. "I do love you," she whispered. "So much it frightens me at times. Not because you frighten me," she was quick to respond to his intake of breath. "Oh, not because of that. You have become the center of my world, and I love being with you. Seeing you work with the people, seeing you act as a physician and bring healing to people's lives. But it makes me wonder..."

Matt's lips were sun-kissed soft against hers. "Makes you wonder if you should be with your own people? The People of the Air?"

Laurin nodded. "My grandfather said I would bring balance—his prophecy so many years ago. It didn't mean what the men of the tribes thought it would, not with you and I being a couple. We are a couple, Matt. I don't deny that for an instant. But where does my responsibly to my people end? If I make a complete commitment to you, your place is here, on the Pacific coast. You *can't* give up your position, and I would never expect you to."

"And I don't want you to feel you have to choose between your nature and our relationship." He stroked his fingers through her hair. "I had no idea this was bothering you so much. I guess I'm guilty of thinking the mystical connection between us will make our relationship easier."

Laurin laughed softly. "It does make things more interesting at times, that's for sure."

Matt tweaked her nose. "I don't want to cut off our discussion, but we need to return to the *Stormchild*. Can we pick this up back at the ship?"

Laurin kissed him as sweetly as she could. "I'm sorry I've kept this from you. You're right, the only way we can figure it out is together."

She reached for the lifejacket and he held out his hand. "I'll take care of the kayak. Why don't you fly home?"

A streak of pleasure hit her. An opportunity to glide on the currents overhead was exactly what she needed right now.

"Are you sure?"

"Of course. I can tie her on behind my mine." He laughed, the bright sound dancing around them as she rushed to strip off her clothes. "Besides, any excuse to get you naked is a good one."

He stroked a finger down her breast and grinned as her nipple responded instantly to his touch.

"Stop that." She giggled, giddy from excitement. From his touch and anticipation of the flight.

"Why? Can't you fly when you're turned on?"

"Oh, I can fly, but if you get me going too much I'm not leaving until you deal with me." Laurin wiggled her brows and Matt licked his lips in response.

"Not sounding like a threat to me, woman." He kissed her breathless then set her back on the ground, slapping her bare butt cheek and pushing her forward. "Go. I'll take care of your needs back in our bed. One session of sandy sex a day is enough."

Laurin blew him a kiss, bent her knees, then launched herself into the air as she shifted.

She changed into her favorite form, the golden eagle she'd first taken as a child so many years ago. Her magic let her shift to any of the People of the Air, but this was the one that felt the most comfortable. It brought great pleasure to extend her wings to reach another inch, tilting a wing tip to catch the proper angle to rise rapidly into the air. She wheeled to peer down at Matt, already far below. He bowed deeply in respect, and her heart constricted afresh. If she'd been in human form, tears would have filled her eyes.

Matt had given and given, and even now showed how pure his love truly was. She called out his name, her eagle's tongue tangling the word until all that echoed out was a cry of passion.

He was her mate, but he was not of her people. At ten years old her destiny had been proclaimed, but not explained, and now as she turned to travel the paths of the sky back to the single-masted ship they currently lived on, Laurin wondered just what the final answer would be to her dilemma.

There didn't seem to be an easy resolution, with her heart torn between fulfilling her responsibilities to the People of the Air, and her unwavering love for the shaman of the People of the Sea.

Chapter Two

"Wait. Did you remember to carry your digits to the top of the equation?" Laurin's voice floated over to him and Matt smiled. All day, as he'd puttered around the ship and taken care of small tasks, Laurin had been hooked up to Skype and the satellite, checking in with students scattered across the Pacific Inside Passage. The firm control she kept over all of the children amazed him. Her sheer joy in working with them made him even more aware that what she did was important, and he needed to find a way to support her as she carried on.

As they moved forward.

He leaned back on the wheelhouse wall and watched her. A strand of hair had fallen free from her ponytail and dangled over her forehead. Her hands moved animatedly, eyes bright. Enthusiasm painted every part of her.

Her confession yesterday had thrown him. He'd known something was wrong, but as the shaman of the water people, he only had so much ability to sense her emotions. They had a connection that went deeper than the average couple, but that didn't let him actually read her mind. Only enough to let him sense her unease and confusion. He hated to have made her feel that way.

If it took letting her go back to her people to solve the mystery, he would let her go. Only he would also accompany her, and be there to support her. Somehow surely they could find a way to take the steps that were needed, and take them together. There had to be a solution other than one that made them go their separate ways.

He didn't want to be without her. The thought of her leaving him forever was enough to make him crazy.

"Matt, is there any more coffee?"

She leaned against him, rubbing her neck, and he reached up to take over the task. "I'll make a fresh pot. The old one must be like tar by now."

"I'm sorry, I got caught up in a few things, but the kids at Dufferin Island finished the group project I assigned them, and they all had to show me the pictures they took. I think I looked at every one of their Facebook pages." She tightened as she stared at her watch in shock. "Oh my, is that really what time it is?"

Matt kissed her forehead before tugging her into the cabin ahead of him. "Yes, that's what time it is. You want coffee or a glass of wine? Since you completely missed cocktail hour."

Laurin handed him a wine glass out of one of the tiny cupboards in the galley, and he reached for the bottle willingly.

It was embarrassing she'd lost track of time like that. "I could have sworn we just had breakfast. Why didn't you tell me I needed to stop?"

"Because you were working, and there was no need. Besides..." he handed her the filled glass, "...if you get it all done today, maybe you can take tomorrow off. We have a few more days before we're due at the next settlement."

"I think a day off is definitely in the picture." She sipped the wine and relaxed back on the corner seat. "There's not a lot left to do with the students anyway, not until the start of the next semester. And the ones who aren't on semester break will just work through what programs I've set them on. We can take a couple of days."

He shook his head. "It amazes me how you do that."

"Do what?"

"Teach so many subjects. How do you get your brain to flip from advanced anatomy to basic math?"

Laurin laughed. "Matt, how do you know if it's a physical ailment or a spiritual one?"

"I just..." He paused, then joined in and laughed with her. "Hey, that's not fair. It's not the same at all."

"It is. I simply do the next thing. That's all you do, right?"

He sat across from her. "I'm awed by your skills, that's all I'm saying. You're so good with the children. Far more patient than I am, at times."

"I don't know about that—I've seen you around them. But yes, I do love children."

Something caught inside him. One of his initial reasons for not getting involved with women from among the water people was to avoid a repeat of his own fatherless childhood. He wanted a family of his own, and as he admired Laurin, the dream seemed to be growing closer with every day that passed.

She blushed. "Why are you looking at me like that?"

He hesitated. Did he want to freak her out? A gentle shrug of his shoulder. She deserved the honest truth. "I was imagining you with my child."

The flush of red spread to her brow, her eyes widening. She opened her mouth as if to speak, then licked her lips. He let her have the time she needed until she dropped a hand on top of his where it rested on the table between them.

"Someday. I... Oh God, I'm speechless."

He lifted her hand to his lips and kissed her knuckles. "I

love you, Laurin. I'd love to have a family with you. But *someday* is a good enough answer for now."

She placed her wine glass on the table and came around to his side, crawling up to straddle his lap. His body reacted as always, going from semi-aroused to instantly ready for her. Since the moment he'd laid eyes on her, he'd wanted her. Now having the layer of love wrapping the physical desire made their relationship that much better.

They needed to make the next step.

He accepted her embrace, closing his eyes to simply feel her hold him. Take in the sensation of her torso touching his, her lips making contact and sneaking away like an erotic game of hide and seek. Against his cheek, his eyes. Her warm lips brushed his forehead. He tightened his grasp on her hips and nudged her higher so he could bury his face between her breasts and breathe in her scent.

The ache in his groin he pushed aside, wanting to drive them both mad enough with anticipation that when they did make love that evening, it would be even more spectacular than usual. Laurin wiggled closer, pressing her breasts to his mouth, and he bit through the layers of fabric. Hmm, she wasn't wearing a bra, and her nipple tightened to a peak under his lips. The sounds she made as he teased her—his brain was liable to shut down completely, and he'd eagerly throw his plans for a slow seduction out the window, again, if he wasn't careful.

Far too addictive—that's how he found her touch. Her taste.

Instead of carrying her to the bedroom and ravishing her, he slowed. Lowered her into his lap and kissed her. The heat of her sex pressed against the ridge of his erection, but he held her still instead of letting her ride him. She complained and he swallowed the mutterings, his tongue sliding against hers. Wet kisses that eventually led to uneven breathing, with repeated caresses of hands over shoulders and backs.

"I want you..." Laurin whispered.

He laughed softly. How often was he the one to slow them down? "Later. We need to make some arrangements first."

She leaned away, surprise in her expression. "Now?"

"Now. I'm not sure how else you think I'm going to get to the Rockies. It would take a long time to swim there."

Laurin stared at him, her warm body nestled close, her fingers tangled in the hair at the back of his neck. He doubted she even knew she had continued to caress him.

"To the Rockies?" Sudden awareness hit her. "You're coming too?"

"If that's okay with you."

She squeezed his face between her hands and kissed him, hard, pulling back to grin at him. "I had no idea you'd join me. Are you sure?"

Matt nodded. "I want to be there for you, and I'd love to meet your family, if you're okay with me coming along. I promise not to take over—you can call the shots."

Her look of delight faded slightly. "There should be no troubles, none that we can't handle. I'm sure all the tribes have heard we're together now, so there should be no more fistfights over me."

"Well, I don't mind if I do need to offer a little convincing. Wherever or whatever is necessary."

Laurin wiggled off his lap and paced the tiny galley area. "I don't even know where to start dealing with this...nebulous sensation haunting me. I mean, it's just a feeling I have that whatever I'm suppose to do still has to happen."

"Can we speak with your grandfather?"

She froze on the spot and twisted back to shake her head. "I can't believe I didn't think of that myself. Of course we can. And there's the shaman, and..."

He wouldn't have been surprised to see her bounce up and down in her excitement. It hit him—she'd been gone for over two years. It was one thing to have left home to move on with your life, but she'd left on the run. Matt took a deep breath and kicked his own butt for not having thought of it sooner.

"Go on, grab your computer and we'll book flights from Vancouver. Once we finish the next stop on our tour, it will be time to put the *Stormchild* into dry dock for the winter anyway. She's too delicate a creature for the winter storms. We'll need to switch to a sturdier vessel until the spring."

Laurin pulled her computer off the shelf and set up the satellite link. "We can fly into Calgary, and I'll get my parents to pick us up."

Her hands danced over the keyboard as she arranged things, but it was her continued babbling that made him grin. Her delight and excitement was contagious, and as they booked flights and arranged for the trip, he could only hope that somewhere in the midst of the adventure he wasn't setting up for an event that would tear them apart forever.

Hands, strong and firm, caressed her back, sneaking over her hip, and pulled her naked body tighter to Matt's warmth. She nestled against him willingly even as she felt the twinges from their sexual romp the previous night. When they'd finally gotten all the details into place, Matt had taken her to bed and made love to her—an almost frantic rut that she'd thoroughly enjoyed, but wondered where his head was.

That had been the first session of many over the rest of the evening. He'd plied her with food and wine, then stripped her down and taken her on the deck of the *Stormchild* as the sun set on them. He'd moved her to the shower on the deck and washed her clean before carrying her back to the berth and loving her so thoroughly she felt decadently used this morning.

Whatever had gotten into him, she wasn't about to complain.

Except when he reached around to cup her breast she stilled him, catching his wrist in her fingers. "You're insatiable."

He planted wet kisses on her shoulder blade. "Is there a problem with that?"

Laurin laughed, pulling away. "I want to brush my teeth. I need coffee, and then if you still have any sexual mojo left to take care of, I'd be happy to oblige."

Matt sat up in the bed, the thin cover of the quilt tangled around his thighs. The firm line of his abdominal muscles disappeared under the edge of the fabric, and she moved quickly to grab her toothbrush. The sooner she felt human, the sooner she could investigate that intriguing line—with her lips and tongue.

"That's a fascinating expression you're wearing," Matt teased.

She waggled her brows at him and escaped the room before she forgot about things like personal hygiene and morning breath, and let him ravish her again.

By the time the water had boiled, she felt ready to face the day, her face washed, teeth cleaned. Matt had joined her at the sink, his hip nudging her repetitively until she realized he was doing it on purpose, and she laughed.

There was something so right about being with him. Maybe this whole trip back to the mountains was a mistake. Should she just accept that her life was here on the ocean? Why was she dragging Matt across the country to face questions that might have no answers? A trip home to visit family—that part would be wonderful. Her mother would love Matt.

It was the nebulous sense of responsibility she felt to her people that threatened her and Matt's life together.

The haunting cry of a bird of prey broke the morning stillness. Laurin stiffened, Matt tensed at her side. He leapt ahead of her to take the steps up onto the deck two at a time. She followed, grabbing the long shirt that hung on a nearby coat hook and slipping her arms into the sleeves awkwardly as she scrambled to reach the deck.

Matt stood at the stern near the railing, staring into the sky. His shoulders squared, body braced as if expecting a fight. She followed the line of his vision and gasped. A huge golden eagle circled above and her heart leapt to her throat. Kilade? How had the man found her again? Were the tribes still keeping track of when she shifted to her avian forms and using that to find her?

It had been months since Matt had fought her people, and she'd felt certain they were no longer searching for her to take her powers for their own. But above—clearly she'd been mistaken about at least one of them. Laurin stared at Matt. He'd defeated Kilade before, but she'd hate to have him fight again and again if the man continued to ignore no as an answer.

"Matt, use your shaman magic this time. No he-man heroics, okay?"

He kept his gaze directed skyward, but she saw his mouth curve into a grin. "Yes, dear."

Laurin came to his side. "I have no idea why he's here. He said he accepted our partnership. He can't possibly think I'm going to change my mind."

Vivian Arend

Matt shook his head, one arm sneaking around her waist and pulling her to his warmth. "Something feels different. Are you sure it's Kilade?"

All her anxiety knotted into a ball and unraveled. *Could it be?* She stepped forward and cupped her hands to her mouth and called out as loud as she could. "Kallen?"

The eagle dipped his wings and Laurin grabbed the railing, sheer delight racing through her. Meeting Kilade again would have been a nightmare, but Kallen was another story altogether.

She swirled to face Matt. "It's okay, it's Kallen, he's my friend."

She lifted her arms to the sky and gestured the giant bird down. It had been years since she'd seen him. He was huge, the wingspan of his eagle form covering over eight feet as he spread them wide and angled his way downward, spiraling toward the ship. As she watched, she remembered the sensation of riding the wind currents, seeing his minute wing adjustments as he made course corrections. Kallen pulled up hard, back winging with his talons extended to grasp the railing beside where she stood. The force of the wind hit her squarely and pushed her hair from her face, pressing the fabric of the thin shirt tight to her skin.

Laurin stepped closer and reached out a hand to stroke his head in greeting as the tribes did at home. He preened against her palm, his bright eye catching hers, and a tiny flutter of remembered heat hit. Of all the men of the tribes, Kallen had been the one she'd admired the most, with his mesmerizing gaze, his sculpted muscular body. The only one she'd had any interest in getting to know more intimately. When she'd chosen to run away, it was Kallen who she'd been reluctant to abandon. But with his brother and him both vying for the leadership of his tribe, he had been as much of a threat to her as any of them.

"What does he want?" Matt growled.

Laurin startled at the sound of his voice. Guilt shot through her that she could even think Kallen desirable after having spent the past night, and months, in Matt's tender care. She slipped away, snatching her hands to her chest. "I'm not sure."

Matt stepped in front of her, and the eagle jerked away, scratching his talons along the wood railing as he retreated from the shaman. "Stay still," Matt ordered.

Kallen dipped his head, watching cautiously as Matt touched his head, not as delicately as Laurin had. The two males froze in position, and when Matt released Kallen, a string of light curses rose from his lips.

"What's wrong?" Laurin eyed Kallen, concerned that some dire illness she couldn't see had struck him. "Kallen, shift—tell me what's the matter."

Matt spun and grabbed her by the elbow, dragging her toward the wheelhouse. "He can't shift, that's the problem."

"What?"

"He's been cursed. As far as I can tell from first touch, someone laid a geis on him and he's unable to shift until it's lifted."

Laurin had never heard of such a thing. She stopped, turning to face Kallen. "Can you cure him?"

Matt tugged on her arm. "Come below."

"Matt, what are you doing? Why are you acting this way? Is he contagious?" It was the only thing she could think of. Why else would she be herded back into the ship, her lover's face stone cold and emotionless?

He paused and shook his head in frustration. "No, it's not something you can catch, and...I'm sorry." He dropped her elbow, scrubbing his fingers through his hair in frustration.

"For what?"

"I need you out of the way for a bit."

That made no sense at all. "Matt, tell me what's going on. Why are you acting like this?"

Matt spat out the words. "He wants you, okay? That's why he came here. He's been looking for you and thinks you can cure him."

"Can I?" She glanced over his shoulder at where Kallen clung to the railing. "Tell me what to do, and I'll do it."

"You can't heal him, I have to."

"Then...why aren't you healing him?" Laurin cupped Matt's face in her hands. The peace she associated with Matt had vanished. Instead as she stared into his eyes, the blue depths were dark, his face twisted with anger and something shadowy. "Matt, please, just tell me what's wrong."

He squeezed his eyes shut and for a brief moment the calm of his magic touched her. It swirled away faster than she thought possible, and anger and fear poured into its place.

One step back broke his contact with her, then another, before he looked up. Longing and bitter fear colored the fringes of his magic. "I'm sorry. I've never...felt like this before. I can't heal him until I find my balance."

His shirt flew in one direction, his pants in another as he stripped.

"What are—?"

"I'm going for a swim. I can't..." He broke off the words and hauled her against his naked body, kissing her fiercely. Possessive, heated, as if he was storing up her memory in that instant and might never touch her again. Laurin clung to him as she returned the kiss, striving to understand. Longing to provide whatever it was he needed.

When he let her go, her heart pounded. From arousal, from fear. "You're leaving me?"

"Oh, God, *no*." His voice broke. "Not leaving, just... I'll be back. And with everything that is in me, I pray you'll still be here when I return."

Chapter Three

Guilt speared through Matt harder than he'd ever felt before in his life. He raced for the edge of the deck, forcing down the urge to lock Laurin up and tuck her away from the sight of her fellow air shifter.

One foot hit the railing before he leapt over the edge, waiting until after he hit the water to shift. He wanted the shock of the cold, hoping it would knock some sense back into his brain. Seconds later he dashed away as an orca, a killer whale. An image feared by the human community, but he should have chosen an eel. It would have been more in keeping with the deep emotion now bubbling up from within.

Jealousy ate him. From the moment Laurin had announced her intentions to go home, he'd fought the emotion. Denied its existence. He did understand her need to be there for her people. His responsibilities as shaman—he'd been born to them as well. The magic had come unasked for, and he'd accepted it as his duty and privilege to serve his people. He would never deny her that. But knowing she felt torn between the mountains and sea, and accepting he might have to give her up... That part burned.

He twisted in the water, increasing his speed as he raced away from the boat. The water welcomed him. Cradled and held him as he escaped from what he had no control over. Oh God, the spike of pain that hit as he thought about her response to recognizing Kallen. He'd felt her desire, her interest in the other shifter, and he'd never expected how much it would hurt.

His people weren't normally the jealous type. Sharing lovers was common, accepted. But not for him, not Laurin.

She hadn't intended on causing him pain. It had been an honest reaction on her part—and that's what made it all the more hurtful. He knew he wanted no one else in his life, no one but her. He'd sensed that almost since their first meeting.

She hadn't had the same reaction, and perhaps it was because they weren't meant to be forever.

Maybe even now she would shift and accompany the air shifter home. She'd been looking for a way to get involved and help her people—it seemed a logical place to start. With someone she admired, someone who leapt to her mind as desirable.

Matt mentally cursed and dove deeper, trying to outrun his tormented mind and soul. He refused to think about it, just pushing his body to the point of exhaustion, hoping to find the peace of the ocean.

How long he swam, he had no idea, but eventually the stabbing pain within him dimmed. Either he grew numb, or the sea was administering its peace on him. Finding a way to soothe his troubled heart. He turned, watching the ocean floor more closely, examining his surroundings instead of flying past like a torpedo bent on destruction.

He was a shaman. He *healed*—the gift was not his to withhold and administer as he pleased, but as was needed. To turn his back on that responsibility was impossible to imagine. Kallen needed to be healed, and Matt would do so to the best of his ability.

As soon as he accepted that truth, a wash of energy filled

his body. Renewed strength filling his torso as he moved steadily back to the ship. The tight bomb-like sensation in his chest eased. Sadness and guilt that he'd allowed his jealousy to intrude on who he was pressed in momentarily before the ocean answered again with a healing touch.

Oh God, he was being restored by the waters of the Pacific.

As shaman, his powers flowed from the water. Gave him the strength to heal and bring peace to all of the family of water shifters. The power had been a responsibility he had welcomed, but the ability to serve others had occasionally been a touch of a burden as well. He shifted back to human and hung suspended in the current off the small island he circled. The bright blue of the sky was muted as he looked up through the salt water and accepted the caress of the ocean. He'd never been held like this before—ministered to by the sea whose people he served.

It was like receiving a gift for once, instead of being the one to bestow it.

His head broke the surface and he rolled to his back to allow the sun to warm his skin. Cradled in the waves, Matt released the last of his troubles, crying out like a penitent in a confessional. He didn't want to lose Laurin. He feared she would choose her own people if given the chance. He didn't want to return to being alone, unloved except for what he could provide through his magic.

The water washed away his fears. Accepted them, acknowledged them, but then fed him back enough magic to soothe him inside.

He was not alone. Never, was he ever alone. A million voices of the People of the Sea carried to him, blurring together along the water's surface. Beneath the waves, the non-shifting kin called to him as well—the dolphins in their pods, otters and the seals, and far to the north the sea lions and even the great whales. They didn't understand his worries about *alone.*

They were always there.

He gave thanks for their love and comfort, and turned to swim for the *Stormchild.* A spark of inspiration hit—and his heart grew lighter with hope. He would do what was right, but he would also do everything he could to make his dream a reality. That included fighting to keep Laurin in his life.

Matt reached the ship, his mind finally clear and his soul far more peaceful than when he'd left. The slap of the rope ladder as it hit the hull drew his attention upward to see Laurin's concerned face staring over at him. He made the wobbly ascent to reach the deck only to be attacked by a huge fluffy towel and a death grip of a hug.

She clung to him, the warmth of her body bleeding through the towel and heating him. Even more, the strength of her grip on his shoulders as she stared into his face, the concern in her eyes and then the meaningful kiss she planted on his lips—it hit him forcefully, and he accepted it as another blessing.

Then she made a fist and thumped him on the chest, hard, and he swore.

"What was that for?"

"You scared me to death." She pushed him away, arms crossed in front of her, chin tilted defiantly. "What the hell was that all about? You raced out of here like the devil himself was on your heels."

She was right—he'd been chased by the devil's curse of jealousy. Matt dried himself, looking around quickly for their guest and not seeing him anywhere. "I'll explain in a second.

Where's Kallen gone?"

"He's sitting at the prow. I can't talk to him in human form, and your reaction to his arrival scared me enough I wasn't about to shift when you weren't here. I still don't understand what is going on."

"I'll explain. First, let me do what I can for your friend."

Matt found his discarded shorts on the deck and pulled them on before he called out Kallen's name. A golden head appeared over the roof of the wheelhouse. Matt pointed before him. "Come. Let me see if I can lift this curse."

The giant bird landed on the deck and Matt knelt at his side.

"Do you need me to do anything?" Laurin asked.

Matt gestured her back. "Stay out of range. I don't sense anything malicious attached to the curse other than it's blocking his ability to change, but just in case."

A soft kiss landed on his shoulder followed by the sound of her footfalls as she slipped into the wheelhouse where she could watch and remain protected. He smiled at her. Laurin kissed her fingers and he sensed her good wishes.

Before him the eagle cried, soft and low. Matt laid his hands on Kallen's head and gathered his magic, wrapping it in a circle around the two of them to protect and contain whatever might burst forth as the curse was lifted.

Within the sphere, moisture gathered—a component of his water magic. He drew from his abilities to attempt to wash clean the curse, peeling away layer after layer like a rotten wallpapering job. Clumsy, some of the layers. Others brilliantly applied. All of them foul with ill-intent and the desire to cause Kallen harm.

Time meant nothing. Matt focused completely. On giving

from his soul, being who he was supposed to be. By the time his task was accomplished, Matt was sweating profusely, the eagle shaking under his hands. The crisp texture of feathers morphed slowly into slick skin. Kallen gasped with pain. Matt rested his hands on the man's broad shoulders as the shifter returned to his human form, crouching naked on the deck.

They both panted for air, bodies worn from the process as Matt removed the protective circle from around them. Kallen clasped wrists with him, the firm hold allowing them both to stand slowly, providing each other support that Matt wasn't happy to need. He stared up at the air shifter who had at least four inches on him in height.

Matt offered a greeting, hoping to put aside his initial response. "Welcome back, brother. How do you feel?"

The other man took a deep breath and let it go. His mouth opened and—no sound came out. The relieved expression on Kallen's face vanished as he attempted to speak and remained mute.

Shit. Matt held out a hand to the man, waiting for his permission. Kallen nodded, and Matt pressed his fingers to Kallen's throat, feeling for any lingering damage caused by the curse. There was nothing at first, nothing that would make him suspicious, but as Matt continued his investigation, he discovered there was another layer to the curse still remaining. Something strong and complicated, with a sense of both the ocean and the mountains combined.

"Kallen, who did this to you?" Matt asked.

Kallen gestured helplessly.

"Matt? What's happening?"

The concern in her voice was back and Matt motioned urgently. "Go below, and find a pad of paper or something."

As Laurin scrambled for something to write on, Kallen held

179

out a hand. It was a peace offering if he'd ever seen one. A way of showing his gratitude, and willingness to let Matt take charge.

Now if only Matt didn't want to tell the man to leave immediately. The complication of keeping the air shifter around any longer than necessary played havoc on Matt's only recently calmed jealous streak.

"Who among the air clans could have cursed Kallen—with enough power that the curse is multilayered and more than your average shaman can cure?" Matt asked Laurin as she returned, passing the writing pad to the air shifter.

"Someone high ranking? Kallen is in line to lead the Assiniboine people. Well, him or his brother."

"The brother you were afraid of? Who I fought back in June?" He felt her tense even as he reminded her.

"Yes, the same. Only Kallen isn't anything like Kilade. If I had to trust anyone, it would be Kallen. When I was young, he stopped the taunting more than once when my family visited his. My grandfather made us stop over at all the tribes every year. Since we didn't know why I was *Hawáte*, able to boost other's powers, he insisted I learn everything possible about all the People of the Air."

Matt ignored that for a minute, focusing on the issue of Kallen. "His father—would he be powerful enough to arrange this curse?"

Kallen grasped Matt's hand again and shook his head.

"Not your father...but someone from your tribe?"

Kallen turned to the pad of paper but before his pen touched the page, Laurin spoke up.

"It was Kilade, wasn't it?"

A curt nod. The air shifter's shoulders drooped, his massive body full of misery.

They sat in silence at the tiny portable table on the deck, Kallen folding his bulk behind one side, Laurin to his right. Matt watched warily as he took a seat only a foot away. Kallen's gaze seemed to flick back to Laurin involuntarily time and time again.

The layers of curse within the curse—Matt had never experienced such a thing before. He knew it was possible, but the casting would have taken a huge toll on the person. He highly doubted Kilade had the power on his own—he must have convinced others to assist him, including someone from the People of the Sea. With two or more people establishing the curse, it was incredibly complex.

And the cure? Virtually impossible.

Laurin touched Kallen's shoulder—just the touch of commiseration. Matt had seen her do that same thing to a child when offering comfort from a fall or during a difficult lesson. The pain cut hard though, and he had to bite his tongue to stop from ordering her to get her hands off the man. They looked so connected. Even with the variation in their coloring—hers light, his dark—it was obvious they were both of the air clans.

He closed his eyes and tried to find that peace. The offering of the ocean he'd only so recently received.

"Can you tell us anything else about what happened? Or why you've come to us? How did you know where to find me?" Laurin asked all the right questions, and Matt let her take charge. Partly drained from his earlier healing, he let himself mentally drift as he waited. Kallen's pen scratched lightly on the page.

He wasn't sure how long he had been daydreaming. The touch of Laurin's hand on his made him open his eyes. He clasped her fingers tight, not wanting to let go. She smiled, squeezing back before pushing the pad of paper his direction. As Matt moved to read the message, Laurin touched Kallen's shoulder again to get his attention.

"We'll do what we can to help you, I promise." The familiar cool wash of Laurin's magic flashed in a new and unexpected manner, lighting them with a bright incandescence that left spots before Matt's eyes. She shot to her feet in an instant, back against the mast, fear on her face. "What was that? Was that…me?"

He'd never felt her power react like that before. She always insisted she didn't have magic of her own, just the ability to bolster another's. Not once in the past two months during their experimenting had she ever initiated anything he couldn't do on his own. It had to be her responding to something—in Kallen?

Cold dread poured into Matt's heart. He stared at Kallen in horror.

"What did your brother do to you?" Matt demanded.

The written message Kallen passed over provided little information about the actual curse. Two weeks earlier, Kallen had been ambushed during a walk and woke in his avian form. The rest of the revelations in the note turned Matt's dismay to an even greater consternation.

My brother made no pretense of innocence in the attack. Kilade bragged he would now take leadership of our people, and there was nothing I could do to stop him. He told me to find Laurin. Said she was the only one who could cure me. But I see no way for that to occur.

I thank you, Shaman, for giving me back my human form. I had met with two other healers of the air clans before seeking you, and neither of them was strong enough to help me shift. I will continue to search for a cure. I refuse to remain as a mute—I must find a way to return to my tribe and take over from my brother. This deceit proves he is not a worthy leader for them.

"Why would Kilade tell you to see me? I have no healing powers. And if he was the one to curse you in the first place, why offer you the cure?" Laurin moved to Matt's side, crawled into his lap and he curled himself around her, protecting as best he could.

"Kilade had a deeper reason for coming to fight back in June." Matt stared across the short distance at where Kallen watched them carefully. "He actually quit before we were done. He seemed pleased to discover Laurin and I were partners."

"He said he wanted to be sure you were strong enough to defend me," Laurin pointed out.

Matt thought back to the fight. The air shifters who'd wanted to take control of Laurin's abilities had come to claim her as a mate, and he'd fought them, letting it be known in no uncertain terms that her choice was the one that mattered. His suspicions regarding the exact nature of the curse grew.

The situation wasn't improving.

Kallen leaned back on his stool uneasily. His dark eyes took in every move across from him. Matt's reservations wavered as he considered how he would feel if their roles were reversed. It had to be a horrible position—to be totally dependent on others' goodwill for something that hugely affected not only Kallen's future, but his tribe's.

"What if you can heal Kallen?" Matt asked Laurin. He turned her face toward him, ignoring the hope that flashed in Kallen's eyes. "What if you do have the ability, with my help?"

The eagerness she felt was plain to see. "Then I would cure him, of course."

"There's no of course to it. Not everything is simple, Laurin."

She narrowed her gaze. "What are you not telling me?"

Kallen waited, silent and still. Matt hesitated. He had to push past his fears. If this was meant to be, he had to be strong enough to face it himself. "Do you remember how to make your magic rise to the surface?"

She nodded.

"Stand up."

She slipped off his lap and stood beside the table. The wind flicked her long hair around her face and he'd never seen her look more beautiful. "What do I need to do? Am I going to try to cure him right now?"

Matt shook his head. "This is just a test. Give Kallen your hand."

The air shifter eyed Matt, as if asking for permission. Did the man know what was potentially on the horizon? Matt gave a slight tilt of his head, and Kallen accepted Laurin's fingers into his, his large hand engulfing hers.

"Now what?" Her voice trembled.

"Bring your magic to the surface. Touch Kallen with it."

The wind increased around them, like a localized storm had settled on the deck of the ship. But other than that—nothing. Both Kallen and Laurin turned their gazes toward Matt, disappointment in her eyes, resignation in his. Laurin pulled her hand free and clasped them together behind her back.

"It didn't work."

"I didn't think it would."

"What? Then why did you have me—?"

"It's not enough. Your magic alone is not enough. Neither is mine."

Her face lit up again. "So if we work together, we can cure him?"

"I think so."

She thrust out a hand to Kallen, eager and willing. "Give Matt your other hand, Kallen," she ordered.

Matt took it slowly. Kallen wrapped his fingers around hers. The stirring of her magic began again, and this time Matt added his power to the mix. Poured healing into Kallen's body. He tried his hardest, because the alternative was going to be shocking for Laurin to consider, and leaving Kallen cursed was becoming less of an alternative with every minute that passed.

She truly did care for the air shifter—that was clear.

Around them the flash of magic sparkled in the air, although the slow exchange of energy he always felt when his powers were used was almost nonexistent. Something was happening, but not much, and it was Laurin who first dropped her hand from Kallen's and muttered in frustration.

"I can feel it, Matt. I can feel my magic trying to help, but it's like there's a wall. I've never—"

She sat back, frustration and disappointment written on her body. "I'm sorry, Kallen. We tried."

The shifter dipped his head and reached for the pad of paper.

Thank you. If I might spend a few hours resting before returning to the mountains, I would be grateful.

"Of course you can stay. Are you hungry? Matt? I should go make us a late breakfast."

"Thank you, Laurin." Matt made sure he kept his touch light as she came to his side and kissed him. He couldn't resist

185

holding her close for an extra moment, drawing strength from the contact.

Then he was alone with the air shifter, and his internal moral battle reached the pinnacle. He looked across the short distance to Kallen, trying to see the man that Laurin knew. Someone from her past, maybe someone from her future. If she'd stayed in the mountains, she could have ended up mated with him. He was strong—both physically, and in the ways of the air shifters. Although their people were different, Matt sensed the power inside Kallen and knew him to be nearly his equal. Matt's edge came from his connection to the water—the power not his own but shared from the ocean herself.

He raised his gaze to meet Kallen's and the knowledge hit him like a wall of a tsunami.

"You know there is still a chance we can help, don't you?"

Kallen hesitated, then nodded.

"Why didn't you tell Laurin?" Matt's soul ached. Why hadn't he instantly told Laurin either?

It took a while for Kallen to write out his answer. He stared at Matt for a long moment before passing the notepad over.

Kilade told me specifically, and with a great deal of glee, what it would take to cure me. He also informed me that you would never allow it to happen. I have no wish to hurt Laurin, or challenge you, that's not why I came. I did hope you could break at least the first part of the curse, and I'm grateful for your help. Now that I have had the chance to see her again, and know that you are indeed caring for her, I will leave and find another way to be healed.

Matt used his shaman gift to search the air shifter for

truth. What he found was nothing but goodwill toward himself, and a deep admiration for Laurin. The second emotion made Matt's throat tighten. It wasn't love he sensed—more an infatuation combined with a great deal of lust.

Kallen wasn't in love with Laurin, just wanted her. Funny how that actually made Matt feel better.

The other shifter rose to his feet, the towel wrapped around his waist all that covered him. Matt could see why Laurin would have admired the man—he was powerful and strong in body, and it seemed, extremely kind in nature.

"What if I told you there's still a chance for the curse to be lifted?" The words burst out, surprising both of them. Kallen's eyes widened and Matt laughed in spite of the insanity of the situation. "It's not as foreign an idea amongst the water people as it is for your tribes."

The air shifter sat down with a thump, muted hope in his eyes. He scrambled for the pen.

I would never dream to presume. While the situation would be unusual for me, I will admit I have always admired and desired Laurin. But I don't want this at her expense, or at the risk of your relationship.

"At least you admitted you want her. Don't lay on the heroics too thick," Matt muttered. The frown on Kallen's face showed his confusion. Matt waved it off. Damn, the man was a shining example of virtue. "Just a warning—I won't insist on her participation. In fact, she's got to understand completely what the cure will take, and be the one to initiate it. Will you agree to that?"

Kallen nodded.

"I'll explain the situation to her after we eat. I guess you'll be our guest for a few days. There's a spare hammock you can rig up to sleep on deck."

Kallen rose again, bowing deeply to Matt before coughing and pointing to the towel. His raised brow and slight smile made Matt realize just how ridiculous he was being. "Yes, I'll find you some clothes as well. Because even if I'm going to allow you to make love with my partner, I don't need to see you naked all the time until it happens."

Chapter Four

It was the first time the ship had ever felt too small. Matt led her into the forward berth immediately after their meal was finished and proceeded to shock the hell out of her.

He lay stretched out on the mattress, his chest bare. The weather was warm enough that all he wore was a pair of knee-length khaki shorts. She sat on the edge of the mattress, letting her appreciative gaze roam his body.

He returned her admiration, his fingers trailing down the side of her cheek, trickling over her collarbone. The brushing tease lit a warmth deep inside. His voice when he spoke was lower than usual, not quiet as if to avoid Kallen overhearing, but husky and needy, like he was a second away from jumping her. "You were brave to try to cure Kallen earlier."

"Brave? Matt, he's a friend. If I can help, I want to."

"What if it takes a lot of energy to heal him?" Matt warned. "Are you prepared for that?"

Laurin leaned back on one elbow. "Is that why we couldn't do it before? I'm not strong enough?"

He shook his head as he tugged her closer, rolling onto his back with her draped on top. She lay uneasily, intensely aware that on the other side of the door, Kallen remained at the table looking over a pile of magazines. While they had eaten, Matt had asked him to stay for the night, and although she was happy to have a little longer with Kallen around, being in the bedroom with Matt right now seemed somehow...dirty.

"You're strong enough. It comes down to the method of releasing the magic."

Hope rose inside. "Really? Can you teach me how to do it the right way?"

He stroked her hair back from her face, tenderness in his touch. "Why are you so eager to cure him? He's the brother of someone who scared you to death the last time you met."

"Kallen isn't like his brother. He's a good man, Matt. I didn't spend a ton of time with him, but what I did, and the stories I've heard, made me admire him."

Matt's eyes darkened, changing from the bright blue of the ocean under the endless summer sky to a storm-tossed sea, fraught with potential violence as it headed unstoppable toward shore. "Then we'll cure him. As soon as you're sure."

She pressed up, ready to head back into the galley. "I'm sure. What do we need to do?"

His arms pinned her in place. "Join our magic. Through you."

Laurin froze. "Excuse me?"

Matt didn't allow her to retreat. In fact, he rolled again and trapped her under his body, hand cradling her face. "I'm going to tell you simply. The magic is built in layers, and this Kilade of yours has found a curse from the mountain people powerful enough to steal his brother's voice. But he mixed it with a curse from the sea, and that means neither of our people can cure Kallen alone. We have to be completely united to cause any effect."

"We are united, aren't we? Don't you want to heal him?"

"It's not enough, Laurin. Want is one thing, but power is

another." He stared at her, the centers of his eyes dilating. "Remember the fertility ritual we witnessed? Remember the woman at the center of the celebration and how she took both men into her body? That's what a cure will take, Laurin. The magic of the sea poured *through* you into Kallen."

He waited. Her pulse had increased the entire time he spoke as the images from the ceremony returned to her— sensual and erotic. It had been one of the most incredible nights of her life, but she still couldn't think back on it without blushing.

This time she pictured herself as the center of attention instead of the woman. Two sets of hands on her body. Matt's familiar and heart-pounding touch. Kallen's firm body pressed to hers, exploring and caressing for the first time. Both of them, working together to bring her to ecstasy.

Her mouth instantly went dry.

"You want me to have sex with Kallen?"

Matt swooped in and took her lips like a wild animal denied food for weeks. He ravished her mouth, thrusting with his tongue and settling his body on hers so she felt his hardened shaft against her stomach. His touch moved everywhere, driving up her desire without a conscious thought. The gentle caresses of moments before vanished as he took ownership of her. Pulled a response from her, made her entire body ache for him to fill her sex with the full length of his cock and drive the madness of his words away.

The drag of his teeth down her neck made her cry out. Pain, followed by unspeakable pleasure hit as he shoved up her T-shirt and bit her nipple through her bra. He crawled over her, arranging her limbs where he wanted them, biting and licking, pinching and sucking until the room spun and she gasped for air.

"Matt, oh my..." He ripped off her clothes and raised her hips in the air and thrust his tongue into her body, nipping at her clit, laving her sex until a climax exploded from her. She bit the back of her hand, striving to muffle the calls escaping as her body shook with release.

Matt snatched up her hands and restrained them over her head, wrists pinned together in his strong grasp. It left his other hand free, and he caught her chin, turning her face toward his. He spoke softly, but clear, loud enough that if Kallen was listening, there would be no doubt that he could overhear.

"Do I want you to have sex with another man? There's a part inside me that says no. Never. I want you to be mine, and mine alone." His gaze dropped over her body, lust filled, possessive. "Your breasts are mine to enjoy and admire. To bite and suck until you squirm under me and beg for me to give you more. Your lips are mine. To kiss softly like a gentle wave, or to take like a winter's storm until they throb from my touch." He traced her mouth with his finger. "Your mouth is mine—not only to kiss, but to press my cock into, filling you intimately, letting you pleasure me until I can't stand it any longer and spill my seed."

Laurin shivered, arching up hard as he stroked his fingers down her body, caressing one moment, scratching his nails over her sensitive skin the next.

"I love to give you pleasure like that," she confessed. Whispered, only for his ears.

He grinned at her, a wild look in his eyes. "Your sex is mine. The taste of your cream, the squeeze of your muscles. The gasps that escape from your throat when I work my way in—all mine, and I don't ever want another to experience what you share with me."

He touched her, fingers circling her labia. She was soaking

wet from simply listening to him. When he slipped a finger into her depths, she breathed out a sigh. Matt thrust slowly, one more finger added. He twisted his hand and the spiraling motion hit something inside that made her gasp. Even as his hand moved, he had leaned forward and now stared into her eyes.

"That's the one part of me. But there's another part..."

He kissed across her cheek, butterfly soft. The illusion of a touch. Laurin attempted to clasp him, but he had her locked in place, hands still frozen to the mattress above her head.

"Another part of me longs to see you in the throes of a climax and be able to watch your face from a distance. I want to feel your pleasure increase exponentially as not only one pair of lips suckle your breasts, but two."

His hand moved relentlessly. As he spoke, he stretched up her arms a little farther, pressing her breasts upward.

"I want to see another man admire you, but only if in the end I know that no matter how good he makes you feel, how much pleasure you receive from him, that it's me you love and want forever."

She teetered on the brink, needing just a little more. "Matt, please."

"Please, what? Shall I open the door and let Kallen watch? Would you like—?"

"No!" Even the thought made her shake.

He rose over her, his fingers slipping from her sex, the hard tip of his cock nudging her folds. He held her in place with his body, wrists still trapped. She was helpless, controlled, and yet there was no fear but an overwhelming sense of urgency inside her demanding she satisfy his need.

Whatever he required at this moment, she was willing to

give. All the time they'd spent together, all the conversations and quiet evenings, all the wild moments in bed and more unusual places, meshed together into a tapestry filled with color and sound.

"Take me. Oh God, please, Matt. I'm yours, just take me."

He thrust and she screamed out, his hard length splitting her in two, and she'd never been so filled before. Her heart pounded, her breasts ached. It was as if everything he'd mentioned was there, available. The sensation of his mouth at her breasts—but not enough. His cock thrusting in again and again—and yet somehow she was empty. He slid over her, skin on skin, lowering his mouth to hers, and she kissed him eagerly, offering her lips, her tongue.

Herself.

Her cries of pleasure grew louder, and still he didn't stop. He released her wrists, growling as he spoke. "Keep them there."

She clutched her fingers together and clung to the sheets, wanting to obey, fighting the dire need to hold him tight.

He reached down and lifted her hips into the air and thrust even harder, and she called out his name, waves pulsing through her as her orgasm rocked her. Matt slowed, sweat trickling down his brow, his eyes glittering as he let his gaze roam over her. A series of aftershocks shook her as he lowered her to the mattress, his hard length still buried within her sheath. His body shook as if he fought for control before he withdrew without reaching his own climax.

She struggled to catch her breath. That had been the most unusual and wild lovemaking session yet, except for the fertility ritual she'd witnessed. Even thinking the words brought the images back, and when she felt a touch between her ass cheeks, she tensed.

Matt stared at her. "Even here, Laurin. I want this to belong to me as well. I want every part of you to know my touch and feel my possession." He pressed in a circle against her, wetness on his finger. She shuddered and would have closed her eyes, but he shook his head. "Watch my face. Witness how much this means to me."

He slid a digit in, opening the tight muscle, and she struggled to relax. Matt worked his finger in and out slowly, the sensation strange, but not unwelcome. The rest of her still buzzed from her climax, and when he leaned over and touched his tongue to her clit, her head nearly hit the ceiling.

"Too much. No, no more. I can't..."

"You can. Accept the pleasure I give you. Take me—into your body, and your heart."

She was going to die from an overdose of ecstasy. One touch led to another. He licked her intimately, adding to the fire building in her core. The sight of his head buried between her legs, dark hair against her light limbs, combined with what he was doing, drove her crazy. He wouldn't stop, not until she fisted a handful of his hair in an attempt to pull him away long enough to smooth out her breath.

He moved like lightning, grabbing a tie-down strap from where it usually secured the cupboard doors. The firm black material was looped around her wrists in an instant, his fingers slipping along her wrist.

"Matt, what are you doing?" Each word took extraordinary effort to say, desire wrapping her in a tight cocoon of need and want she feared might never get answered.

He paused after slowly tugging on her wrists as he looped the free end of the strap through a wall bracket. Matt swallowed hard, rasping out the words. "Tell me again. Tell me to take you. That you're mine, any way I want."

She wiggled, brushing his naked body with hers the best she could, and his eyelids fluttered, face tightening. On the other side of the door, Kallen still sat, unless he'd escaped to the deck of the ship. He would have heard every one of her cries, could probably imagine what they were doing, and the thought didn't embarrass her, but made her hot. Heat poured from Matt, his hunger for her clear. But over his desire, the powerful need for her to surrender to him was obvious.

Did she want this? She tugged on the straps securing her wrists, and the flash of desire in her core nearly tipped her over the edge into another orgasm.

"Anything. Everything. I'm yours."

Relief filled his eyes briefly before being washed away with lust. Something cool and wet touched her. His finger pressed into her ass again, easier this time. Smooth and slick. Somewhere he'd found lubricant, and when the stretching touch on her back passage grew she gasped.

Flat on her back she could see his every move. He adjusted her position, pressed her limbs higher, knees wide to the side. With her arms trapped overhead, there was nothing she could do but comply and allow him control.

And watch. Examine every nuance of expression that flitted over his face. Every word that escaped his lips fell clearly on her ears. Words of love and desire, and possessiveness. She shivered and he caught her gaze with his own.

"You're mine."

The tip of his cock touched her body. Pressure increased and she consciously relaxed, drawing strength from the look of love in his eyes. Heat, pain, something between the two streaked through as he opened her. It was strange and wonderful, and she couldn't remain silent another second. She called out his name, her voice echoing against the walls of the small room. There was nowhere on the ship that wouldn't have heard her, and she was glad.

She wanted Kallen to know that here, now, Matt was loving her so completely she could no longer restrain herself. The sensation of Matt filling her body grew in pleasure as he worked his way in. One slight rock after another, each one touching her in new places, not just in her body, but her soul. She'd given to Matt before. Offered her body, but this—far more intimate, far more complete.

And the pleasure? "Oh my God, how can this feel so good?"

His groin met her ass and she shuddered. He leaned forward and suddenly her hands were free.

His eyes—incredible. The light in them dazzled her. "We belong together. In all ways. At all times."

He dragged his hips back slowly. A series of ecstatic shocks spread through her lower limbs. It wasn't just where they connected that felt the pleasure. Inside her sex, over her breasts. Her entire body was a part of the lovemaking and she needed completion. Needed to have him truly take her. Laurin planted her feet on the mattress, and the next time he pressed in, she moved as well, increasing the pace and the hardness of the thrust.

"Matt...more. Harder." It wasn't enough. She was in danger of igniting into a pyre, the lingering embers of passion heating her everywhere. She cupped her breasts, pinched her nipples. Anything to make the moment she craved arrive.

Matt's grasp on her hips increased, his fingers squeezing the soft flesh as he raised her slightly and drove in. Her breath whooshed out, each plunge into her body priming her closer to the breaking point.

Then he leaned over her, one hand resting on the bed, his cock still buried deep. He slipped his other hand between them and touched her clit, and that was all it took for the sky to meet her. She was flying, her entire body a part of the experience. Pulsing around his shaft, his continued drags as she clutched him serving only to draw out her pleasure beyond what she thought possible. His thumb rubbed her clit, her orgasm washed through her core, making her blood pound, her hands shake, her vision blur.

Matt froze, his groin tight to her skin, his shaft buried deep. Their eyes met and he came, the ecstasy on his face setting off another series of tremors in her body. Heat, pressure. His possession of her complete and oh-so-welcome. His arm where it pressed into the mattress beside her body shook, and she reached up and hauled him down, skin to skin. Like a flash fire, sparks exploded as their bodies connected. She shivered with how good it felt to belong so completely, to have been commanded by him for her own pleasure.

She felt cherished as he wiped her clean. Felt treasured held in his embrace as they cuddled together on the mattress. Their breathing still erratic, still shaken by the extreme satisfaction of their lovemaking.

She closed her eyes and soaked in the experience.

When he tugged her shoulder, rolling her to the side, she went willingly. Oh God, his eyes—his eyes glowed like a lightning storm over the water. He touched his lips to her forehead. Held them there. Spoke against her skin so quietly she had to strain to hear.

"I love you, Laurin."

The words blessed her ears and stirred something deep, deep within her heart. "I love you too."

Chapter Five

Somehow a small portion of hell had broken free from the depths of the earth and risen to surround his ship.

Matt sat at the prow of the *Stormchild* staring at the coastline as he tried to decide the proper tack to take. Below him on his bed, his heart slumbered. He'd well and truly worn Laurin out, and she hadn't moved when he'd reluctantly crawled away from her warmth. The soft protest that rose from deep in her throat had made his body react, but he had to deal with his uncertainties before the next stage happened or he'd go mad.

He was fairly certain they could heal the air shifter. Kallen's curse, now that Matt had identified it, was one that he should be able to wipe clean. Laurin's ability to enhance his strengths meant a cure was possible. As long as the three of them had sex together.

And not just any sex. Wild, passion-filled, off-the-charts sex linked with magic.

Above him, the sky shifted colors as sunlight reflected off the mountains and hit the drifting clouds. Out toward the west there was a warm haze rising from the ocean, but over the mainland and Interior Mountains clouds gathered, clinging to the peaks. Matt would have given anything to simply sit on the deck and stare at the amazing beauty surrounding him with

Laurin at his side.

He loved her. Wanted her in his life. They had so many questions still to solve, and he had been looking forward to a lifetime of finding the answers. Heading to the mountains with her—all of it was important and still a part of his plans, but now...

High overhead the shadowy outline of an eagle blotted out the sun, bringing into focus exactly what was on his mind.

There was no way to deal with this situation without confirmation that Kallen was completely on his side.

The air shifter descended, shifting on the wing to land lightly in human form on the deck not two feet from Matt. Kallen's wide grin and pleased body language said it all.

"Nice day for a flight. Did you see anyone else?" Matt asked.

Kallen shook his head as he reached for the shorts Matt had loaned him, pulling them on to cover his nudity.

There was no reason to make small talk. To the point, before Laurin woke. Matt wanted to make it clear what was, and wasn't, going to happen.

"Kallen, I love her." The man nodded slowly. "Among the People of the Sea, sex is often treated more casually. The idea of having two lovers or more in a bed isn't unheard of. But it's not what I had planned for us. For Laurin and my relationship."

Kallen grabbed the pad of paper and wrote rapidly, passing over the notepad with a raised brow.

I do not intend to attempt to steal her from you. But I refuse to take a woman who does not desire me.

"She does desire you." The air shifter frowned. Matt sighed, stomping off to the side. He picked up a loose rope from the deck. As he coiled it, he leaned back on the mast, watching Kallen carefully. This had to be a part of the whole. Curing Kallen—that was one part of the picture. Laurin's doubts, and her desire to be there for her people needed to be considered as well. Allowing Laurin a chance to find exactly where she belonged—to the water or the air—was vitally important. "She also loves me. Your brother is an evil genius. He's managed to come up with the only plan that ensures the maximum chance of you not getting healed."

Kallen stared out over the water for a long time before turning to the paper.

Laurin is of my people, but she has never truly belonged there. When she disappeared, I was glad. I hoped she had found a new home. While I do not love her, I wish the best for her. There is nothing I can do to prove it beyond telling you—if it is right for Laurin to stay with you, I will honor that. If she desires to return to the mountains for good, then I will do whatever is needed to make that happen, including take her as a partner. I'm sorry if that angers you, but it's the truth.

Another ache formed in Matt's soul. "You know, this would be a lot easier if you were an asshole, Kallen. I'd simply tell you to get the hell out of here and never have to look at your ugly mug again."

The air shifter grinned.

I find myself enjoying our time together, Shaman. Tell me, do you ever hunt?

Matt laid aside the coil of rope. "What are you thinking?"

Kallen wrote and then strode to the railing, leaving the paper behind for Matt to read.

An animal when hunted runs to safety. Finds the most attractive location. An animal being wooed by a mate reacts similarly—showing their preferences without even saying a word. Shall we hunt Laurin together? Let her reactions tell us what her desires are?

An uneasy peace settled over Matt. He didn't want to like Kallen, but every step the man made reassured him more and more.

"You want us *both* to seduce her." Kallen shrugged, but the heat in his eyes echoed the sensation Matt always felt when he thought about Laurin. "Remember, I love her, and it's still her choice."

Kallen bowed low. A formal, dignified motion that carried years of tradition and respect. He was truly a prince of his people, worthy of someone like Laurin. Matt stared toward the lower compartment of the ship. Only he wasn't going to let her get away without a fight. Even if this battle would be fought on a far more sensual stage than the earlier one with Kallen's brother.

Over one full day had passed since Kallen's arrival and Laurin was ready to jump out of her skin. No matter where she turned, one or the other of the men seemed to be right where she was. Reaching into a cupboard, her arm brushed past a bare shoulder. Bending in the tiny galley to light the burner, her hip bumped into a groin, Matt's arousal instant and noticeable. The weather had turned unseasonably warm, and all three of them wore only light clothing. Shorts and a tank top for her, nothing but shorts for the men. Kallen and Matt had worked around the ship and generally got in her way, no matter where she was.

She had slept in Matt's arms, the door to the cabin wide open to let the light breezes float past. When she opened her eyes, Kallen was standing at the stove, lighting a flame under the kettle. His rigid body was all darkness and light, swaying in the shadows. Strong muscles curved over his abdomen, a trail of dark curls led down under the elastic of his shorts. Laurin watched from under half-lidded eyes, hiding from him, feeling his gaze roam over *her* naked body under the crumpled sheet.

Matt's skin flamed against her back, his hand nestled possessively over her breast. He nuzzled her neck, and instantly she grew wet and ready.

And Kallen watched, eyes black as midnight filled with clearly written need.

She had the power to heal him, but she had to choose. Matt had made that clear. Yet she was torn between loving Matt and feeling guilty she felt desire for Kallen. Even as her lover touched her, stroking her nipple with his thumb, she wondered what it would be like to have Kallen join them. To thread her fingers through his dark hair and draw his lips down to hers. To taste him for the first time, run her tongue along his strong jaw. Drop her face against his neck and breathe in his scent. Pull his muscular body over hers and feel his length fill her sex.

She was going insane.

Out on the deck she fled, looking for privacy in a space that allowed none. Laurin lay on the deck and closed her eyes, her bikini an attempt at modesty when usually she would have lain in the nude.

The heat of the afternoon sun faded in comparison to the

reaction in her body when she heard their footfalls approach. Two sets, walking slowly around her. Pausing at her head and feet.

She opened her eyes slowly, looking up into a stormy ocean of blue as Matt squatted at her head, leaning over. His dark hair fell across his forehead is a smooth wave.

"Do you want to go for a swim with us?"

Laurin sat up quickly. "With both of you?" She turned to stare at Kallen in shock. "You swim?"

He tilted his head politely.

"You've gotten good enough—and it's a warm day. Come on, lazybones, time for a little exercise." Matt reached down a hand to her, and she slipped her fingers into his, wondering why she tingled so hard all over.

Of course, the fact two virile men were staring intently at her nearly naked body had nothing to do with it. No, nor the fact she knew they both wanted to make love with her. Needed to make love with her.

Laurin stepped toward the ladder. She still hadn't worked her way up to throwing herself over the side of the ship like Matt enjoyed. Only her movement was blocked by a rather large, warm body. Her entire front made contact with Kallen's chest, the heat of his bare skin searing hers. She retreated and found herself up against Matt's solid frame, his hands catching her upper arms to steady her shaky body. Wet need bloomed between her legs, instant desire for her lover spreading like a flame over the water's surface.

She leaned back into Matt's support. Maybe if she hid in the forward berth... "Do I have to swim now? The water looks cold."

One of his thighs slipped between hers as his arms surrounded her. A blanket of heat covered her, spilling from his torso. "We'll keep you warm."

We'll? *Oh my God.* She looked forward into Kallen's face and a shiver rolled down her spine at the expression she found there. Need, desire, admiration. She was so intent on finding a reason for the emotions she almost missed when he bent slightly, bowing before her.

Only a second later she realized he wasn't being polite, but removing his borrowed shorts. The muscles of his upper body tapered in at the waist, the bold cuts of his abdomen clear and firm. She tried to keep her gaze from dropping lower, but there was no way to ignore his groin, the way his cock rose from his body, fully aroused.

She'd seen his naked torso when he arrived, but now...she couldn't breathe. Couldn't swallow. Couldn't think.

The air that had been trapped in her lungs escaped as she realized not only was she staring, she was rubbing against Matt in the most provocative manner. Her hands pressed to his thighs as she leaned back, her own body on display for Kallen as she reveled in the heat of her lover's body.

How could she look at one man while in another's arms and want to touch? To taste?

Embarrassed, overwrought and excited, she twirled and buried her face in Matt's neck. Laurin clung to him tightly, looking for a little balance in the midst of the shaking her heart had experienced.

"Shhh, it's okay, love. I'm here." He stroked his fingers over her shoulders, light, easy. She took long, slow breaths and let his peace roll over her like the smoothest of seas.

Laurin pulled away and stared into his eyes. "Are we going swimming?"

She wasn't going to let fear overtake her. She'd come so far, she'd been so strong. This situation was highly unusual, but nothing she couldn't handle. Not with Matt at her side.

His smile lit her inside. "We swim, and show your friend from the mountains how much fun the water can be."

He stepped back and she gasped in shock. He'd untied her bikini top without her knowledge, and the tiny triangles fell to the deck like tired flags in the calm of a storm. Her hands shot up involuntarily to cover herself, but he shook his head slowly, eyes wide with desire and admiration.

"You don't need to cover yourself. I want to enjoy watching you. I want you to feel the water's caress on your bare skin. As if I have a million fingers, each one dedicated to your pleasure."

Oh God, the images. She closed her eyes and the reaction of her body to his words filled her senses until there was nothing but the two of them. Her nipples tightened, breasts suddenly gone heavy. She sensed him move closer, felt his mouth approach her own. His kiss was gentle. Lip to lip, tongues only meeting with the fleetest of touches. In her mind she saw them standing on the deck, suddenly aware of Kallen at their back. His arousal growing as he witnessed them body-to-body.

Embarrassment morphed into something else. Into a new kind of pleasure. Having Kallen watch was—beyond good. It added richness and a depth to her commitment to Matt. She threaded her fingers through Matt's hair and gave back more. Offered herself with enthusiasm.

His hands roamed her body, rubbing and touching and stroking her higher. She was going to need to jump overboard soon to put out the flames licking over her entire torso from his touch. His magic swirled around them. Not for healing, but simply there—a part of him, and a part of her now as well.

When another large hands grasped her hips, she froze in mid-kiss. Matt held her face, cupping her cheeks as he pressed their lips harder together. It was Kallen who grabbed the edges of her bikini bottoms and slipped them from her body, the thin fabric stroking slowly down her legs like an erotic tease.

Her heartbeat raced. Heat from the air shifter's body brushed her from behind while Matt paused his adoration of her lips for long enough to stare at her.

She found herself lost in the depths of his blue eyes. Uncertain how she could want another when the man before her held her heart. Held her soul in a way that she never wanted to be freed.

A single finger stroked her skin. Kallen, smoothing his way up from the sensitive area on the back of her knee, up her thigh. Over her butt, pausing in the small of her back. Red-hot connection jolted through her as he flattened his palm over her lower back. He moved closer, and she felt his breath against her neck.

All the while Matt caressed her inside and out with his gaze. Held her tight with his love and longing.

Confusion, passion, wild desire and complete chaos tangled together in her mind, and it was suddenly too much. She broke free, chest heaving as she struggled to pull air into her lungs.

Matt's face grew unreadable. Kallen watched, silent because of the curse, but she doubted he would have spoke if he could. Two sets of eyes, waiting for her to say what she wanted. Two men whose bodies clearly showed they wanted her.

"I need to fly."

The words burst out of her like an explosion. As if all the sexual tension they had built in her core gathered together to send her propelling skyward.

Matt hesitated, his eyes dark, deep. "Then Kallen flies with you."

God, no. "I need to be alone. I need..." Had to find a way to release the tension overtaking her before she did something she'd regret. Healing Kallen was important, but loving Matt was her future.

Wasn't it?

If she were absolutely certain, none of this would be as difficult.

Matt's deep voice caressed her ears. "I understand, but we've harbored too close to the inland mountains. If Kallen could find you, there might be others and I don't want you to be harassed in any way."

Another jolt shot through her system. Would she ever be free of this upheaval? "You want me to fly with another man?"

His expression smoldered and a million tiny fires lit all over her body, everywhere his gaze touched. "If I could, I would go with you myself. I trust you, and I trust Kallen..." Matt broke for a second, "...trust him to have only your good at heart."

Laurin glanced at Kallen. The man she'd admired for so long stood motionless, waiting for her response. His body hard and beautiful in the sunshine. Jaw solid, but his dark eyes tender, and her throat tightened. The swell of desire that rose unbidden, it had to be wrong.

On her left Matt waited as well, every plane of his body familiar and well loved. He'd shown her the world of the ocean, and given of himself again and again, and yet...

The mountains called.

She turned and shifted, threw herself into the air and caught the minute breezes that changed direction every few feet as she fled from the deck of the *Stormchild.* Flew as if speed could help her escape. Not from Matt, not from Kallen, but from the uncertainty and the frightening thought that she might have to give up her heart to serve her people.

She couldn't turn her back on destiny.

The ship receded rapidly, fading to the size of a child's toy. As the land appeared below her, the air currents changed radically, allowing her to rise even higher near the rugged peaks. A piercing cry cut the air, and she faltered.

Kallen.

He trailed behind, letting her lead. Allowing her the illusion of privacy, but every single second she was completely aware of his presence. Knew when he turned with her, moving subtly into her air space. Felt the fleeting brush of wingtips against hers. She swore his gaze on her back burned, igniting the wick of desire she wanted to deny existed.

He was from her people, and a part of her past. Was he supposed to be a part of her future?

Onward she flew, attempting to find the answer. She had missed the familiar comfort of knowing when an updraft would hit as she rounded a mountain corner instead of the uncertainty of the ocean—she'd yet to learn to read the currents correctly. All she was guaranteed was that at some point in the day, *someone* would get her wet.

The thought made her smile. There was far more laughter in her life these past few years than there had ever been before. The People of the Air were volatile and impulsive, but they weren't prone to many outbursts of joking or hilarity. In the ocean setting, she was guaranteed a slow buildup of joy each and every day.

Kallen touched her again, bolder now. Courting her as he cut in front and displayed a fine skill in flying. If she returned to the mountains with him, she could help rule. Perhaps take some of the lessons she'd learned and teach her people how to have a little more fun.

She admired Kallen even as the remembrance of lessons

triggered an overwhelming sadness at the thought of leaving her students. Heartbreaking grief at the thought of leaving Matt.

It was official. Insanity had set in and there was no clear picture of the right path to take. One moment pulled one way, the next, the other.

Kallen stroked her again and her body reacted. Heat flared between them and she cursed it even as she welcomed it. After so many years of admiring him from a distance, to have him pursue her made her feel desirable in a totally new way. She wanted him, wanted to return home and see her family. Wanted all the past memories that were tied up with fear to be erased and healed with a future filled with serving and loving.

A future without Matt? Impossible.

With that, it hit. The utter certainty that no matter what else needed to happen, it simply had to be with Matt. He was no longer an option but a deep driving need at her core and a vital part of her life. Laurin cried out his name and wheeled. She would go to the mountains, would find a way to serve her people—with him by her side. It was possible for them to juggle the two worlds, especially since there was so much she could teach her people.

She prepared to fold her wings and dive from the heights, returning to where her heart waited for her. The flash of Kallen's wing in her peripheral vision held her back.

Rejecting him wasn't the goal, but accepting him in a totally different way than Matt—that she could do. She rolled, scooping under him and cutting off his wind, making his flight spin out of control briefly. Before he could do more than adjust his balance, she did it again, joy spiraling up in her belly as she considered what they must look like—two mighty golden eagles dipping and drooping like a birds drunk on overripe berries.

She knocked him off kilter three times before he returned

the trick, catching her with his talons and spinning her away. Laughter pooled in her heart. He understood. He accepted. His touch turned light and playful instead of sensual like before and she rejoiced.

Laurin tucked, descending on the *Stormchild* like a bomb. She had to tell Matt before she exploded with happiness.

Chapter Six

He stared after them, the bright backdrop of the sky creating a canvas for their bodies as they rose so high their forms turned into tiny pinpricks of reflected light.

Stepping back as she took this flight was the hardest thing he'd ever done. If only he knew for certain what she would decide. He didn't doubt her love for him—it was her sense of responsibility that stood between him and happiness. How could he fight a battle against exactly what led *him* to be the man he was?

He would never make Laurin choose between him and her people.

Of course, if Kallen hadn't shown up on the scene, it might have made things a little easier. His jealousy this time was far less. He liked the man—damn it anyway. Even over the past day as they'd played games and worked on the *Stormchild*, he'd come to enjoy having another male around. A person who he could be a friend to without being *the shaman*. It was an experience he hadn't known since his days at university.

In spite of admiring Kallen, Matt wasn't about to bow out. If Laurin felt she had to return to the mountains permanently, he would not give up. They would find the answer of how to deal with their dual roles. Because being without her would be like losing his soul.

Matt sat on the deck, gaze still trained up on the sky. Laurin and Kallen had long since disappeared, lost in the shades of green and gray of the Caren Mountain range. The rocky crags hid them, the distance between them growing. And yet—he felt what could only be described as an undeniable tug.

He pulled off his necklace with its minute leather bag. He'd worn it ever since Laurin had given him the prayer stone after their first morning together as a couple. The magic of his people allowed it to go with him when he shifted. He'd never questioned the enchantment—it simply was. Like the tiny sack and its contents were a part of him.

Tipping the bag over, he allowed the smooth stone to fall into his palm. He sensed her through it, knew that no matter where she went, he'd be able to follow her. Some of his people believed the stones could guide them. That it held a tiny piece of home to draw them back to hearth and safety. He knew it was more, that the magic in the stone was not between a person and a place, but between two souls.

He cupped the smooth rock and rubbed it between his fingers. Eyes closed. Picturing Laurin in all her seasons. All her roles he'd come to appreciate—teacher, friend...lover. Partner in discoveries, playmate in their off-time. She'd been a support to him as he served his people, always open and willing to negotiate the differences between their cultures.

He'd learned so much from having her around. Her impulsive hugs and bursts of enthusiasm shook his deliberate approach to life. The way she could flare up with anger and just as quickly offer forgiveness—the first few times he'd been sure he would never be able to understand her. Now he saw there was strength in spontaneity that could benefit his people.

Stillness.

Quiet.

Vivian Arend

From far beneath the waves slapping the sides of the *Stormchild*, he absorbed the peace of the ocean. Breathed it in and allowed it to become a part of him. Waiting, like only the People of the Sea knew how. Water could wear down the mountains, turn them into a soft sandy beach, if given enough time.

He remained at rest. Reached out, sent his love, offered his support to allow Laurin to find her own peace. The wind flapped the furled sails lightly, the deck rose and fell easily.

Tranquility.

Calm.

A change occurred, first sensed on the air. That awareness he had of her ripened, turning lush and fruitful, and his hopes rose. With a rush she approached, lightness and elation surrounding her. He turned his face skyward and laughed as she joined him, shifting back to human a meter above the deck and tumbling into his arms. She knocked him to his back, kissing him madly, warm skin covering his.

"I love you. Oh, Matt, I love you so much. I want to stay with you, and be with you. I know it now, I *know* it..."

And his heart grew a size, filled with her presence and her confession. It was going to work out. He squeezed her tightly before forcing her back far enough to look into her eyes again.

"I love you too."

She grinned, face radiant, the worried creases at the edges of her eyes gone. She scrambled to her feet. "I'm sorry, I didn't mean to knock you over."

"I didn't mind at all." He replaced his necklace, coming to stand at her side. She tucked up to him again, breath warm as it fluttered past his chest. Her hands smoothed in circles on his back, the fiery trickle of desire rising between them. As easily, as beautifully, as always.

214

Laurin leaned in and kissed his chest. "I..."

She turned her face upward and he swore softly. Her magic snapped around them, vigorous and powerful, ready to be unleashed. Held in only by a thread of control.

"Laurin?"

"I want to heal Kallen. I don't want to hurt you, but I care for him. As a friend, and I..." Her mouth opened and shut a few times before she grimaced. "Why is this so hard to say?"

Matt laughed, taking pity on her. "Because even after months with my sexually charged people, you're still a modest air shifter."

She blew her bangs out of the way and nodded.

He tugged her back with him, sitting on the deck head and nestling her between his legs. "Shall I help you say it?"

"Do I need to say it?" she whispered. Fidgeted. Wiggled, her embarrassment clear.

She was adorable. A little teasing wasn't going to hurt. Could lighten their situation even. "I need to know specifically what you want of me—so yes, you need to say it."

Laurin's cheeks flamed red, and she glanced into the sky. Kallen had remained above them. He circled the ship, his wings barely moving but for slight changes in the wing tips. "He's a good man, Matt. But I don't feel anything for him like what's inside me when I think about you."

Happiness bubbled up. It was more than contentment that filled him at knowing he was her first choice. Allowing another to touch her—he could handle it with her full gift of love so willingly given. "Then we should heal him."

She shimmied between his thighs, brushing his limbs with her smooth ones. The familiar tingle of desire that never really left him when she was around returned in full force, his body

215

reacting. He rearranged his position until their torsos connected.

"You said...we need to...make love?"

He nodded.

She swallowed. "You don't mind?"

It was the same question she'd asked before, only the intent this time was so much different. The first time she'd been shocked, dismayed even, that he might allow another to touch her. Now, the interest she felt wasn't an either/or, and he smiled.

"I don't mind that you find him attractive. You need to let your caring for him be strong. It's the only way the magic will work."

He kissed her. Reassured her of his love through the contact. Slowly her body relaxed, her fingers against his chest moving to explore. Slipping over his shoulders, dropping to outline the ridges of his abdomen. Their tongues stroked together, slowly, smoothly, tasting the pleasure of each other as if it were the first time. She nibbled her way along his jaw, tiny flicks of her tongue blessing his skin and heating his blood. Together again as they belonged, the whisper of an earlier lovemaking session meshed in, and he let the thrill of it spill back to her.

They were so much more than mere lovers.

It would be so easy to pick her up. Scoop her and carry her back to their bed. But in light of what needed to happen—and how tiny the berth truly was—Matt chose to stay on deck. Somehow, it was proper. The backdrop of the mountains rose behind them, the sunlight sparkled on the water. Both their spirits could be at peace here, and the magic could heal Kallen.

Matt drew Laurin to the side, leading her carefully to the foredeck, stopping to open a chest and pull out a thick blanket.

Her eyes widened, and she flicked a glance skyward, suddenly nervous again. He grinned.

"Kallen landed already. He's behind you."

She twirled. Laurin covered her breasts with an arm, one hand falling in an attempt to maintain her modesty as Kallen stalked toward them. Matt held his breath. Was she really ready for this? It was one thing to have lost her inhibitions during the summer ceremony a couple months ago. There had been the wild pulse of the community egging her on.

Now, she had to make the deliberate choice to put aside her reticence.

Kallen slowed. Stopped a respectful distance away. Dipped his head, and waited.

Matt checked his own internal barometer. He'd been torn apart by jealousy not even a day ago, but try as he might, he could muster no grudge or anger toward the man. All his jealousy had been washed clean by the strength of Laurin's love.

She turned to face him. Straightened her shoulders, lifted her chin. The soft cough as she cleared her throat made him hide his smile. *Brave, brave woman.*

"My love, shall we heal our friend?"

A flash of magic shot out with her words, lighting the area, fluttering the flags on the rails. Her eyes widened and her mouth formed an "O" as she blinked rapidly.

"I think we had better, before you use that wild magic and we find ourselves flying in the *Stormchild* to your Rocky Mountains."

The slight fear in her eyes faded, and she mouthed the words *I love you.* He winked before stepping forward and bowing to Kallen. Matt turned Laurin slowly, seeing the air shifter's response as he admired her fully.

There were no more words needed. Matt kissed her cheek, then pressed Laurin forward, his hand on the small of her back directing her unsteady limbs toward Kallen.

The emotional roller coaster made her heart pound out of control. It was one thing to come and confess her love for Matt. Every cell in her body acknowledged that truth easily. To take the step and admit her admiration for Kallen? And now to witness his desire for her as well?

It was unnerving and frightening, and so sensual she could barely breathe.

He approached, wary. Like a hunter stalking a deer. She felt every bit the hunted, and yet the desire to turn and flee rapidly disappeared. The rising urge to envelop him in her arms and eat him alive grew faster than she thought possible. Laurin peeked over her shoulder. Matt had laid the blanket on the deck, and he stood to the side, watching. The most incredible expression covered his face.

Desire for her was plain. No denying it at all. But there was interest even now in his gaze as it shifted back and forth between her and Kallen, and she remembered his words from their loving the previous day. How he would like to see her in another man's arms, receiving pleasure, if he knew her heart belonged to him.

It did.

She took another step toward Kallen. His muscles flexed in anticipation as she approached. His dark eyes flashed, gaze dropping over her body. Another pulse of heat flushed her and yet she paused. There was something just not right. No matter how much she admired the man...no. Not like this. Her hand rose of its own accord to reach for her lover.

"Matt?"

There was no hesitation. He was there, his fingers meshed through hers. He stayed behind her, his mouth making urgent contact with the tender spot beneath her ear. Goose bumps formed instantly over her entire body. Her nipples tightened, her core grew wet and she ached for him to take her.

Before her, Kallen waited. His expression hunger-filled. His body taut and ready—fight or flight. Or a hard driving desire to join with her. Kallen's face revealed more than he probably wanted. That it wasn't simply his need for a cure—her power alone—that attracted him. With Matt at her side, she could do this.

She held out her other hand to her fellow air shifter, and the final distance between them disappeared.

He let his fingers envelope hers, gentle yet firm. With his right hand he touched her cheek, a fleeting, delicate caress as he stared into her eyes. At her back, moisture painted her skin as Matt licked her shoulder blade. Kallen's nostrils flared momentarily, as if sensing the fresh flush of arousal Matt's touch had provoked.

Kallen leaned forward and kissed her. Lips solid and confident in the contact. Laurin waited for guilt to arrive, but in its stead, a blaze of yearning ignited and she was lost.

The kiss deepened, his tongue stroking hers, lips and teeth involved. Hands caressing, tugging, lifting. Swirling and coaxing a response harder and hotter than she'd expected.

Because it wasn't simply Kallen. It was Matt as well. His mouth, *his* hands, his attention focused one hundred percent on her. Giving her pleasure. Stirring up the sexual flames inside to the point there was little left to consume without her burning up completely.

How, with only their hands on her skin, could they trigger

219

such a response? Their mouths, the faint brush of the air from their lungs, the gentlest of touches from the pads of their fingertips—none of them in themselves overpowering, but as a united front?

Urgency grew great in her core. Needing—something more—and Laurin let her head drop to the side. A slow twist rubbed her torso against the smooth skin of Matt's chest as he pressed intimately close. Near enough his arousal was obvious, hard and hot in contact with her hip.

Kallen's breath sped up as he cupped her breast, warm air feathering over the peak a split second before his lips made contact. He sucked, and pleasure dropped like a heavy anchor from his mouth to the aching place between her legs. Laurin glanced down to watch, letting the eroticism of seeing him lick and suckle drive the experience higher. Her heart pounded, the tingle of her orgasm far too close to deny even after only the short time of lovemaking.

She'd been on edge since Kallen had arrived. Hell, in terms of being sexually needy, her entire world had ridden the height of pleasures ever since she'd gotten together with Matt.

A sudden gasp escaped her lips as her lover scooped her up and lowered her to the blanket, his body covering hers briefly as their mouths met. His taste—so familiar, so enticing—filled her senses. Memories from earlier days together swirled through her mind, and the ache in her body refused to be diminished. He chuckled softly as she kissed him back fiercely.

"I like how you cling to me, Moonshine." Matt's words tickled in her ear, his lips fluttering along the rim as he rolled them to the side. Laurin flushed as she untangled her fingers from his hair. She hadn't realized how quickly she'd taken possession of him. Another body joined them. Kallen crawled alongside her, stretched out at her back.

Trapped between two men—one who held her heart, one who she admired and desired. The last lingering twinges of her modesty fell away, and she smiled, staring at Matt.

"I'm ready." She levered herself up slightly to take hold of the firm muscle in his neck, licking it and suckling. Leaving a mark with her teeth and tongue to show *he* was *hers*. At the same time with her top hand, she reached back. Catching hold of Kallen's hip, she tugged him toward her.

Their response came in a flash. Both men groaned, the utterances rising low and rumbling from deep in their chests. The sounds were primal and primitive, and Laurin welcomed the answering shot of lust that made her wetter than before.

Kallen rocked against her, his shaft heating her skin, moisture from his cock brushing her ass cheek. Matt returned to her lips, hands falling to her breasts to plump and mold them as the heat between them increased. The gentleness of moments before dissipated and the ride kicked up a notch.

When Matt left her mouth and turned to her breasts with his lips, forcing her to her back, Laurin fought to contain her cries of pleasure. That worked for a moment. Just long enough to notice Kallen was no longer at her side. Then her thighs were separated and Kallen buried his tongue in her sex.

"Oh. Oh yes." Flustered, yet needy, she willingly drew her knees farther apart.

The air shifter muttered his approval and increased his pace. His tongue lingered over the increasingly sensitive peak of her clit. Fingers slid over her labia, smooth and teasing. He circled, and circled, rarely dipping any farther into her core. Never enough to make her fly over the edge.

"Bastard…"

Matt lifted his head from where he'd been worshipping her breasts. The tips of her nipples stung, the faint breeze against

221

them cool after the heat of his mouth. He glanced down at where Kallen was tormenting her with pleasure. Matt took a deep breath, shaky and rapid. When he turned back to her, his eyes glowed—*oh God*, the fires reflected in them were powerful enough to nearly make her climax.

"You are so beautiful. So giving." The words floated to her ears through a rising buzz as her blood pumped harder and harder. Matt stared, his fingers circling one breast, then the other, tweaking and pulling her nipples until she wanted to scream. The whole time he watched. Every touch Kallen made must have registered on her face. And when the air shifter finally, finally thrust his fingers into her core, the bright sky behind Matt's head disappeared as her vision distorted. Pleasure was the only thing that registered.

Her climax rocked on, between the encouragement of Kallen's mouth, his steady thrust of into her sex, and the expression on Matt's face as he watched.

Her heart was full to overflowing. Love for the water shaman. There was no jealousy in him, she felt the emotions he shared even now. His delight in seeing her receive the gift of ecstasy from Kallen's touch. His satisfaction that he would have forever in the future to provide more for her. Not only sexually, but as a friend and more.

Tears threatened. Laurin thought she'd managed to contain them, but when Matt stroked his thumb over her cheek, he caught moisture and wiped it aside. He didn't need to say the words; his body and soul spoke straight into hers. Through their intimate connection of minds, he poured out his blessings. Swore his commitment and offered all his love.

That's what the physical desire she felt for Kallen lacked. The element of forever simply wasn't there.

She was a contented puddle on the blanket, and they'd

only begun. Laurin sat up and reached to smooth her fingers through Kallen's dark hair as he kissed her intimately one last time before rising, his face covered with a broad grin. He might not be able to speak yet, but his thoughts were obvious.

"He's feeling a trifle cocky he made you come."

Laurin smothered a laugh and threw her arms around Kallen first, then Matt, hugging them close. "I think you two are the ones still feeling cocky. Shall we do something about that?"

The words were so much more risqué than she would usually utter, and her cheeks felt flushed with heat. Their response was immediate, and the light amusement on the air faded. A sense of anticipation rose. The images she remembered of the woman at the center of two men, being loved by them both, struck again, and she shivered.

Then there was nothing but sensory overload as they turned their complete attention on her. The touch of Kallen's hands over her waist, the flare of her hips. So good as he pulled her to her feet, led her up onto the raised surface of the forward hatch and twisted her away from him. His shaft sat solid as steel along the dip between her butt cheeks. Matt stood in front of her, lifted her chin and took her back up to breathless. Kisses, soft and slow, were followed by his teeth biting into her lower lip, his tongue smoothing the throbbing surface.

As Kallen stepped away, then slipped a finger between her ass cheeks, she stiffened briefly. Matt soothed her, petting her body, dipping his own hand down to stroke his thumb in tiny pulses over her tight nub at the apex of her mound.

Moisture touched her. Not just the liquid from her core coating Matt's fingers as he cupped her possessively. She twisted her head to see Kallen kneeling behind her, his fingers well coated before he laid a tube aside.

She was ready to ask where he'd gotten it, the lubricant,

but when he looked up at her, the words dashed away. She didn't really care. All she wanted was his touch. A touch to echo the one Matt now bestowed on her sex. The aching need to be filled increased, and she widened her stance. Wanting to make this happen.

Soon.

Now.

A fingertip brushed between her cheeks, cold and wet. It warmed quickly as Kallen pressed in up to the first knuckle. Laurin deliberately relaxed as much as possible, but it wasn't easy. Not with Matt lapping at her earlobe, his touch relentlessly taking her back up. When Kallen added another finger she felt nothing but pleasure. After the experience the day before—she wasn't afraid of this. Not even when his fingers were replaced by something far broader. Thick, heated. Kallen pressed firmly forward with his cock until the muscle opened to him.

A low cry snuck out. There was no pain beyond the pain of desire asking for more. Matt held her hips as Kallen entered her, and she stared into the endless blue of his eyes as another possessed her.

There was nothing there that spoke of jealousy. Only her, what she needed. If she'd uttered a single word to indicate she was distressed in any way, they both would have stopped instantly.

What she wanted was more. The sensation of Kallen in her body in such a way—there were no words to describe it. Full, but not nearly enough. Small strokes of pain she couldn't distinguish from pleasure. One rock of his hips after another he worked his way in, pulses blasting from the nerves inside to wrap her entire body in need. He touched his lips to her shoulder the same instant his groin went flush against her backside, and they both shuddered.

Matt stepped before her, his gaze mesmerizing. The touch of his hands, intoxicating.

Wordlessly, he lifted one of her knees, her weight barely held on the remaining single limb. Then she didn't need to support herself at all as Kallen bore all her weight in his hands and she floated in midair, speared on his shaft. Every motion forced her harder onto him.

"It feels...oh God, it feels so good. Ah..."

"Hold my shoulders," Matt ordered, and she hurried to comply. Palms glued to his skin, she wrapped her fingers around and held on for dear life as he stepped onto the platform she'd just vacated, placed his cock between her legs and pulsed upward.

So full, so much. It was both physical and mentally overwhelming. The thought of what they were doing was less intimidating than the why. And the emotions pouring from Matt...rich and full, caring and complete. When his lips brushed her cheek she realized only then that tears were falling.

"Is it too much?" he whispered.

She shook her head, leaned back into Kallen and reveled in the insane gratification sweeping her that two men desired her and loved her so much. "Take me. Use my magic."

She opened herself, the cool source inside her breaking free. She'd always considered her magic like the wind, able to go where it wanted. Usually the only thing it allowed her to do was shift into any of the People of the Air. Now as Matt moved in counterstroke with Kallen, one long drag and thrust after another into her core, the magic refused to disperse. It clung to her skin as if she'd flown through a cloud, tiny droplets of water clinging to her limbs.

Then the magic coated them all. Flowed over Kallen, mixing with his natural magic that allowed him to shift. It swirled forward, and not only mixed but blurred intimately with Matt's, and a sharp rush lit her, inside and out.

The rising orgasm—she knew how her body would react normally to lovemaking. What it felt like to come around a cock buried in her core, in her ass. But this? It was like the climax was ready to pour into her mind and soul at the same time, and the air crackled with potential.

Laurin stared at Matt, drowning in his eyes. Sharing her love for him even as out of the corner of her eye she saw her fingernails dig into the flesh of his shoulders.

Their speed increased, hands firm on her hips as her men anchored her in place. They surged in unison and she shouted. The constant rub against everything sensitive inside ignited a spark, raced along her nerves and hit the powder keg in her core and that was it.

"Now, Laurin, now. Hold on to me, love, and give to Kallen."

The sky disappeared, because there *was* nothing but them. The pulsing of her orgasm as she squeezed them tight. The wash of heat as they joined her, Kallen's body hard at her back, Matt enfolding her from the front.

And the magic? She swore they were flying, suspended somewhere far above the deck of the *Stormchild*. The next instant they were immersed in the power of the Pacific as Matt joined them with the ocean. Dove through her, translated her magic into something the air could accept and...

"Laurin!" Kallen's shout rose to the sky, his voice raspy and harsh and broken as he shook with his release.

Swirling lights continued, the wind whipped around them, but through it all the blue of Matt's eyes gave her a center of calm to cling to. He squeezed them shut for a second as he came, prying them open immediately to wash her in their warmth.

As if the ocean had surrounded her, bathing her with limitless love.

Somehow they ended up on the blanket, all shaking limbs, heat and sweaty bodies. Laurin closed her eyes and let the sun shine down on her and bring another kind of heat, so much less powerful than the one she'd just experienced.

Matt cradled her close. "I love you."

He said it again and again. His lips made contact with new spots after every announcement. Her mouth, her eyes, her cheek, the curve of her neck. Something wet and warm touched her as Kallen returned and cleaned her. She hadn't even noticed he was missing.

She'd been so focused on Matt, and that's how it should be. But now…

Laurin rolled as Kallen sat beside her.

He grinned at her. "Simply saying thank you seems an understatement, but 'My God, that was incredible' seems inappropriate well."

She laughed. "How about I say the incredible part. Wow."

Kallen glanced at Matt. "I understand how tough that must have been, and I am grateful. More than you know."

Matt dipped his head in acknowledgement.

A sudden silence fell, and for one brief second Laurin was floored by where she was. What had happened. Naked between the two of them, she had no urge to cover herself. She wanted nothing more than to stretch and preen. To let them start all over again. Maybe even try a few of the other things she'd witnessed during that ceremony. The picture of taking Matt into her body while she took Kallen into her mouth popped into her mind.

Instantly, she felt a grumble rise from Matt. "What are you doing, Moonshine?"

Kallen swallowed hard. "Is that...from Laurin?"

She snapped upright, sure her jaw was hanging open. "What are you talking about?"

Matt chuckled, and she quivered with anticipation at the tone of it. "You're playing with the dirty pictures again, and this time you're showing them to Kallen as well? Oh dear. *You* are the insatiable one."

She pressed her hands to her cheeks, discovering them red hot to her touch. "What did you see?"

Kallen shifted position and stared over her shoulder at Matt. "I had planned on leaving you two alone, but I'm far more interested in staying. If you have a need for me, that is. More help hunting, that kind of thing."

Matt laughed even as Laurin struggled to understand. "It's up to Laurin. Let's ask her."

They tugged her to her feet. Matt enfolded her in his arms and guided her to the bow of the ship. The sun was just beginning its slow descent toward the horizon, the afternoon gone and the evening stretching out with all kinds of possibilities. He stopped at the railing and motioned Kallen forward. The two of them stood before her, smiles and admiration written on their faces as they turned to face her.

Confusion hit. What were they asking? Did they think she was going to choose between them? She already had.

"Is Kallen completely healed?"

Matt frowned briefly before touching a hand to Kallen's throat. There was the brush of his magic and he nodded. "And you don't have to worry about anyone trying to use that curse again. I left a trace of it behind like an inoculation, tweaking so it will backfire on the caster."

She gasped. "I didn't know you could do that."

He raised a brow. "I probably couldn't, not by myself. But you were fairly spectacular back there, in more ways than one."

Laurin flushed and tilted her chin up. "So what now?"

Kallen bowed slightly. "If you'd like, I would love to experience a few more of your 'pictures'. And anything else you would like to share."

"As would I..." The hunger Matt shared was real, and Laurin's throat tightened. He sent her a wave of love, of acceptance. Of desire to see her pleasures exceeded as she'd experienced earlier. But it was up to her.

Did she want more? Now for play, and not for magical reasons? She glanced at Kallen. He was beautiful and strong, and she would love to fool around a little more. But Matt?

Her heart.

They both stood, waiting for her decision, giving her the final choice after making it clear what they wanted.

There was no denying it, and the words burst out as she forced herself to not make it sound like a plea. "Let's do it."

Kallen nodded once, then dove into the water.

"What? Where is he...?"

"Getting cleaned up. For the next round." Matt grinned at her and to her complete surprise, snatched her up in his arms and kissed her. Her legs supported under the knees, one arm under her torso, she felt like a modern-day heroine.

Except for the naked business.

When he finally let her up for air, she licked her lips. "Hmm, I could get into more of that."

"Of course, after you get cleaned up as well."

He stepped to the rail and she clutched his neck.

"Matt! No, you're not serious." Her protests fell on deaf ears as he tossed her after Kallen. The air whistled past rapidly. She slammed her lips closed to stop the water from filling her mouth, hands slapping the surface as the sharp contrast of her heated skin and the icy water surrounded her.

Bastard. She broke the surface a second later, just in time for the wave from Matt's cannonball entry to wash over her head and send her sputtering. Then he had her in his arms as he drew her struggling body against his.

Interest rose in spite of the frigid temperatures. He held her carefully, his smirking expression lit with pure shimmering gold as the sunlight hit.

"When you least expect it—that's all I'm going to say, Mr. Shaman. When you least expect it..." She kissed him briefly, the salt on her lips mixing with his flavor and making her smile.

"Hmm, okay. But for now? You can totally expect a lot more of this." He rocked his hips against her and she laughed.

"How can you be hard when the water is this cold?"

He tsked in dismay. "Are you cold? I guess we'll have to warm you up."

A second set of hands roamed her body, and every bit of displeasure fled.

"Anything you want, Laurin. We're yours for the rest of the night." Kallen's voice had settled back into the firm tones she remembered, and the shiver along her spine had nothing to do with the temperature and everything to do with anticipation.

It looked like it was going to be a long, and interesting, evening.

Chapter Seven

The ship moved easily as the morning tide turned, and a small yawn escaped as she stood waiting to say goodbye. She was tired in places she didn't think ever got tired, but wallowing in satisfaction made the lack of sleep all worthwhile.

Kallen leaned in and kissed her. Thoroughly. With enough heat to make her toes curl. At her back, Matt cleared his throat and she couldn't stop from giggling. Kallen smiled against her lips, and suddenly the passion faded into good solid friendship—the main thing she felt for the man.

"He's very possessive," Kallen complained.

Laurin winked. "Sharing me is one thing the shaman doesn't do easily. Didn't you notice that? He totally steals the covers as well."

"Hey, you two." Matt surrounded her with his warm arm and Laurin sighed with contentment. Boxed between two men who cared for her—how could she feel anything but ready to take on the world?

Kallen leaned closer and whispered in her ear. "We would have been good together, but you and he are better than good. You are in balance."

A shiver stroked her skin. Enough with the omens. She laid a hand on his cheek and gave him a final quick kiss. "I'll miss you, Kallen. Be safe—and when we come east, we'll stop and see if there is anything we can do to support you against your brother."

The air shifter nodded, his eyes sparkling at her before he turned to face Matt fully. He bowed formally, then grasped hands like kin. "When you stand in need of me, I will return. Or..." his gaze darted back to roam over Laurin's body and she blushed, "...if you ever wish to play some more, I'm available."

Matt pushed him on the shoulder, grinning good-naturedly. "Go on. Find your place, but know you are always welcome in our home."

Kallen stripped off the shorts he'd borrowed, raising his brows briefly in Laurin's direction before shifting and rising on silent wings into the air. She tucked under Matt's arm and listened to the sounds of the ship, the noises of the ocean and wind making the ropes sing. Waves splashed against the *Stormchild*'s sides in a rhythmic pulse that matched the timing of Kallen's wings in motion. Sunlight sheered off him, and they watched without speaking until his giant eagle form disappeared from sight.

Laurin was going to miss him. Strange how quickly they'd become friends. It wasn't just the sex, as intimate and wild...and totally exhausting as it had been.

"Regrets?" Matt asked softly, his fingers caressing the back of her neck as he nestled her body against his.

She shook her head.

"You could have ruled the mountains with him."

That wasn't an appealing thought. "Too much like work. The air clans are all about power and hierarchy. You people of the sea know how to play more. And besides, he's right—you and I—we bring balance."

Matt turned her to face him. "You to me, and I to you. But I think it's even bigger than just between us. Our people are going to benefit from the lessons we can share. It's been too long since the air and the water shifters have worked together."

Laurin laughed. "Some of the lessons are going to come as a shock."

He grinned and nodded. "We're still planning to go to visit your people in a few weeks, correct?"

"Of course. I think we should stop in at the Assiniboine tribe first though, and cast our support behind Kallen's leadership." It felt wonderful to be certain of at least a few things. "I'm not sure what we'll find, but I now believe that whatever I am supposed to do there, you're supposed to be a part of it."

He stroked the back of his knuckles against her cheek. "I'll go anywhere you need me to."

Together.

She led him toward the wheelhouse. A sudden thought struck her. "Wait a minute. Kallen said he'd return when we stand in need of him? What was that about?"

His gaze heated. "Remember your science, teacher."

She shook her head. Nothing came to mind.

When he reached for her and cupped a breast in his hand, his lips descending to tease and nibble on her neck, she still wasn't sure what he was talking about, and she was growing less interested in finding out. Laurin returned his advances, attempting to bring their mouths back in contact. He laughed at her, eluding her attempts.

"Still not sure? When we want to start a family, we have some twisted magic to perform—air and water combined. And Kallen can act as our third."

Laurin froze. "You're... Oh my God, you're right. That's true."

She couldn't get pregnant right now. Didn't want to get pregnant yet. But someday... Wild images from the previous night poured through her mind. Bodies tangled, the dual possession. Four hands caressing, two mouths teasing her passions higher.

Matt groaned and clutched her close. "Hell, woman, you're doing it again. Making me see all the dirty things I want to do to you." He grabbed her hand and forced it against his groin, and she grinned at the obvious power she held.

"Not dirty. Passionate, and perhaps creative. Exactly what I need and want."

He grabbed her by the butt and a gasp escaped her lips as he manhandled her against the door. His strong body forced her back, his arousal a clear and solid temptation as he ground against her. She countered by building a scenario in her mind. Her, naked on the bed. Rolling to her knees and reaching between her legs. She highlighted his entrance to the room and poured a healthy dose of what she felt for him. The lust and the desire, of course they were a part of it. But more importantly, the love, and unending need for his presence in her life.

She packaged it together and then let it free. Her magic flared around them, hitting him solidly. His head fell back slightly and he groaned, receiving her gift, her passion.

Accepting her.

As well as accepting all the crazy things that went along with being partnered together. His responsibilities to the People of the Sea would constantly change, as wild and far-reaching as the ocean itself. Of her future amidst the air shifters—she had no idea what to expect.

They'd face it together.

His hands shook as he stroked her body, dragging his hands up her torso until his fingers were buried in her hair.

Matt tugged her face up to meet his gaze full on.

He spoke, the words inducing a shiver up her spine at the need in them, the dark hunger barely contained. "I love you. All of you. With all of me."

Laurin drew from deep, deep inside her to confess the truth. "My life would be so much less if I hadn't met you."

His face lit up. "Through the storms and the peace, I'll stay with you."

She nodded rapidly, choked with emotion. She had to say it—had to let him know. "Matt—you bring *me* balance."

The ship rocked under them, but his grasp on her body kept them upright. They both smiled, joy filling up to the top and overflowing. The wind picked up, singing through the high wires, rattling the lines and the sails. Laurin's hair whipped around her face and she pulled it back.

Matt brushed his lips against her cheek then pushed her lightly toward the stern to start the chores that had become second nature to her with practice. She watched him for another second, admiring his smooth gait forward. His lingering glance over his shoulder in her direction heated the warm spot in her heart like a glowing ember.

They moved silently, working as a team. Tightening straps, pulling in anything that could be lost if the storm raged too hard. Then they retreated below to the compact cabin. It was more than enough—the place filled with memories from the past months. Filled with hopes for the future. Laurin tilted her head toward the forward berth and Matt grinned as he crowded her into the tiny space. They stripped off each other's clothing before their lips and bodies moved together in a perfect harmony. Outside the *Stormchild* the seas turned rough, rocking the ship. She was solid enough to withstand the challenge—well-enough built to face even an unexpected storm or two.

Laurin felt the connection, strong, wild. This time it was Matt's magic that filled her, overwhelmed her. Brought her to the place that she knew she never wanted to leave. In the center of any storm, she'd found the place she belonged. With Matt—somewhere between both their peoples. One day, one adventure at a time.

About the Author

Vivian Arend has hiked, biked, skied and paddled her way around most of North America and parts of Europe. Throughout all the wandering in the wilderness, stories have been planted and they are bursting out in vivid colour. Paranormal, twisted fairytales, red-hot contemporaries—the genres are all over.

Between times of living with no running water, she home schools her teenaged children and tries to keep up with her husband—the instigator of most of the wilderness adventures.

She loves to hear from readers. Send an email to her at vivarend@gmail.com. You can also drop by vivianarend.com for more information on what is coming next.

It's not every day a woman faces down the bitch
who owns her man's soul.

Dark Currents
© *2010 Mima*
Elementals, Book 1

Xia is sick and tired of having her ass served to her every bloody night. Exhausted, she soldiers on, working the Scottish dream beat alone, seeking to identify those who plot to awaken Aqua, one of the four slumbering elements. Should Aqua fully open her eyes, she won't be happy until she picks her teeth with the bones of the last human on earth.

When an assassin tags Xia, her new guardian arrives—a seal shifter linked to the very element she fears. Adam is certain that Markos, Xia's boss and sometimes lover, is putting her in unnecessary danger. But Xia has tasted the inhuman cruelty that is Aqua and will do anything to stop her, even relive a terrifying, perilous spell.

Now that Adam has been assigned to protect her witchy spirit wanderings, Xia has to trust him. It isn't his power or ability she's uneasy about, but the fact he'll have to take all the pain meant for her.

Then the Chamber ruthlessly deploys Xia and Adam in a dangerous ritual. Adam can protect her body and defend her mind...but nothing can safeguard her from the backlash of the world-changing knowledge she discovers.

Warning: This adventure is blatantly Scottish and dives into save-the-world sex with two of the hunkiest magical men you'll ever meet.

Available now in ebook and print from Samhain Publishing.

PUBLISHING

It's all about the story...

Romance

HORROR

www.samhainpublishing.com